Clarice Berry Castle

Ballerina Dreams

Cloudberry Castle

Ballerina Dreams

Janey Louise Jones

 Kelpies

Kelpies is an imprint of Floris Books

First published in 2012 by Floris Books

© 2012 Janey Louise Jones

Illustrations © Moira Munro

British Library CIP data available
ISBN 978-086315-920-6
Printed in Great Britain
by CPI Group (UK) Ltd

For ballerinas and dreamers
everywhere

1. Christmas

It *is* lovely living in a castle. Especially as it is also a ballet boarding school and ballet is my absolute favourite thing in the whole world. This ballet school is owned by my parents, because the castle was a gift to my family from a lovely old man, Dr Campbell, who used to live here. We took care of him when we lived in cosy Holly Cottage at the bottom of the hill. Christmas time makes me think about Dr Campbell and getting the castle in the first place, because it all happened at that time of year. Getting our own castle felt like being in a dream, except you never wake up, and the dream goes on happening. Finally it sinks in that it's real: the castle is truly your home.

My family lives in a private flat on the first floor of the castle. In the school holidays I live there too, in my own room. But during term time I sleep in the school part of the castle with my good friends, Tilda, Catriona, Polly, Leo, and lots of others who board with us – up in the girls' dorms. We have great fun up there, and it gives me some privacy from Mum and Dad, and my little brother and sister, Hamish and Sorcha, too. When we first opened as a school, Mum and Dad were stressed and seemed to be on my back the whole time, but everything smoothed out a bit by the end of the first term. Phew! Thank goodness.

I do love my new ballet school friends, but, when the Christmas holidays arrived, I couldn't stop thinking about my oldest and best friend, Mallie Lennox, who has always lived nearby, at Tullyacre Farm. Mallie and I did everything together before Cloudberry Castle School of Ballet opened for business. She was with me every step of the way when I decided to persuade Mum and Dad to open a ballet school. But that was back when we went to Lochvale Primary School together, and to Mrs Miller's ballet classes in the village too, so we saw each other every single day. I don't go to Lochvale School anymore, because Mum and Dad employ school teachers at the castle for all the ballet students. That means I don't see Mallie. We tried to meet up a couple of times during the first term, but there has been so much pressure here at Cloudberry, it hasn't worked out. When all the ballet school distractions stopped for the holidays, I realised how much I was missing her.

I made her a *Swan Lake* Christmas card and cycled over to the farm to give it to her. It was so nice to see the big grey stone farmhouse with all the Lennox bicycles and footballs sprawled around the front door. But there were no cars there, and when I rang the bell, there was no reply, so I just pushed the card through the letterbox. Before I left, I called "hello" around the farmyard, because sometimes her brothers potter about there – every time you see Rory and Finn they look filthy, and smell of dirt and manure. But there was no answer.

"I'm so out of touch with Mallie now," I thought sadly, "I've got no idea what she's up to these days – I didn't even know they were going away."

However, I did see a gorgeous horse's head poking over the stable door. "Oh, Mallie has a new pony," I thought. He was stunning. A shiny chestnut thoroughbred, from what I could see, with a white blaze down his nose. A plaque on the door read

MICKEY

"Hey, Mickey," I said.

But when I approached the stable door, the pony went crazy, rearing and bucking wildly. Seriously, I thought he was going to bash down the door and come charging around the yard.

"Whoa there!" I said. "It's okay, Mickey. Shh. There, there."

He went to cower at the back of the stable. I could see the white of his eye. The poor pony was obviously terrified. I backed away carefully to cause him as little stress as possible, and headed sadly away to Cloudberry, hoping I might hear from Mallie in the New Year sometime, when she got home.

Our second Christmas in the castle was magical in lots of ways. Okay, it wasn't *quite* as magical as what happens to my heroine, Clara, in *The Nutcracker Suite* ballet – but almost.

The Nutcracker has been my favourite ballet ever since Mum read it to me when I was little, and played the music too. Clara gets to do wonderful dances. In the story, Clara's godfather, the toymaker, gives her a nutcracker for Christmas that is carved as a little man. And he gives other toys as well. When Clara comes downstairs in the middle of the night, she finds that the toys and Christmas decorations have come to life! Clara saves the nutcracker man from the nasty King of the Mice, and he turns into a prince and takes her off to the Land of Sweets. The Sugar Plum Fairy is ruler there and she also does some amazing dances. I would love to dance *The Nutcracker* one day. Mum has promised to take Sorcha and I to see *The Nutcracker* at the Scottish Ballet in Edinburgh for a special New Year treat! Can't wait.

Cloudberry estate looks like a fairy-tale place at Christmas time. The hills around us become completely white with snow; it looks like somewhere the Snow Queen might have her ice palace.

Sorcha and I have been talking about making decorations together, so that our family flat will be really Christmassy. I went into her room and flopped on one of her beanbags, ready for a team chat.

"Is it just me, or is this room even pinker?" I asked.

"I've put away all the non-pink things because they didn't match," she explained.

"I see. Well, if it was more pinkness you were after, it's definitely working!"

"Cool!" she said.

"So, about these ideas for Christmas..."

"Let's put all our thoughts on my whiteboard," suggested Sorcha, fetching her pack of rainbow-coloured wipeable pens. "You brainstorm words and I'll write them down."

"Okay. Ummmm... Angels, snowflakes, toys. Fir trees, sweeties, magic," I started.

A big smile came over Sorcha's face.

"What is it?" I asked.

"You know how Mum is taking us to see *The Nutcracker* in Edinburgh for our New Year treat? Well, everything you've just said is in *that* ballet! That's what we should make: Christmas decorations of all *The Nutcracker* characters for our tree!"

"Brilliant idea, Sorch! That will be perfect. And we can bring them out again every year."

"I know, and it's my favourite ballet ever!" said Sorcha.

"Snap!" I said.

2. The Perfect Tree

Really, can you think of a more perfect Christmas story than *The Nutcracker*? I love the fancy gala party at the start, and the intriguing gifts, then the fantastic adventure to the Land of Sweets. And as for the Land of Snow, it's just so lovely that all the perfect signs of winter feature in the dances, like angels, snowflakes and icicles. Oooh, it makes me tingle just thinking about it.

Dad took Sorcha and I out to buy what we needed for the decorations. We found tiny rag dolls in a craft shop in Aberfeldy, then we went to a cloth shop and bought loads of fabrics, especially tutu-style stuff, like tulle and gossamer.

"Come on, girls!" said Dad, as we fussed over teeny sugar-pink beads for the Sugar Plum Fairy's outfit, "it would be nice to get home again this side of Christmas."

Back at the castle we had fun making the clothes for the dollies, mainly fancy tutus. Then we attached a loop of ribbon to each of the characters so we could hang them on the tree. There were, of course, the snowflakes, angels, dolls and icicles. Plus the Dewdrop Fairy, who introduces the Waltz of the Flowers – I love her. And we had dolls of the children: Clara and her brother, Fritz. We made a cute ivory lace dress for the Clara doll, like the sort you see on those Victorian china dolls.

And, to keep Hamish happy, we bought some painted wooden soldiers in smart red uniforms from the village store in Lochvale. He loves marching around as a toy soldier when we dance to *TheNutcracker* music. However, my favourite character, saved for the top of the tree, was the beautiful Sugar Plum Fairy. I worked on her sugar-pink tutu for hours, using lots of layers of net and tulle, and stitching on those tiny sugar-pink beads.

As Sorcha and I were working on the tree decorations, Dad was keeping his eye out on the estate for the perfect tree. We gave him a sketch of the shape of tree we like – just like the one in our book of *The*

Nutcracker: tall and elegant, bushy, but not too bushy at the bottom.

Mum got on with preparing the food, just like she used to do at Holly Cottage, and the kitchen had a delicious spicy smell. She made pies and puddings, a large plum cake, and even some little chocolate truffles and tray-bakes, which we could hardly keep our hands off once we spotted them in the fridge. Seriously, it was like the Land of Sweets in there!

Dad's Christmas specialty is a chocolate log cake. It took him three evenings, but he had it finished by Christmas Eve, when he went out to fetch the huge fir tree he'd found. Once he and Mum had got the tree upright in the great living room of our castle flat, it was just right.

"I've looked at every tree on the estate to find the right one," he said. "So you better jump for joy, or else!"

"Thank you, Dad!" I cried. "It's exactly the same as Clara's tree! Just like the one they put the nutcracker under in the ballet – really dark green and bushy, but not too bushy at the bottom!"

"Yeah, that was the bit that got me," said Dad. "Bushy-but-not-too-bushy. How's a dad to know what *that* means?"

We found a huge ladder so we could decorate it all the way up, because, I am not kidding, the tree must have been about ten feet tall. The ceilings in the castle are three times the height of a normal house. We got Dad to cover the branches in tiny fairy lights. He pretended to get mad with us during that bit, because we kept saying that the lights were not spread evenly enough over the tree.

"Some more down the left side," I told him.

"Right."

"No, left," I said.

"Very funny. I'm running out of patience here," he grumbled.

And so we went on, laughing so much that tears fell down our cheeks. It felt just like the old Christmases in Holly Cottage.

Once we were happy with the lights, we hung the decorations we had made and, to finish it off, we added lots of pink-and-white-striped candy canes and chocolate coins in gold wrappers.

"Those sweets are the only thing I like," said Hamish. "So that means I get to eat those."

"Oh, does it now?" I said. "No stealing – unless you share!"

At last the tree was ready! It twinkled, it

shimmered, it sparkled and our *Nutcracker* characters danced – the tree was as enchanting as the story of the ballet.

"Well, that is the prettiest tree we've ever had," said Dad, when he saw it finished.

"It is quite special, isn't it?" I said. "Let's take lots of photos."

"Wow! You kids are so creative. It's beautiful," said Mum.

3. Ballet Dress-up

Sorcha and I were super-excited about going to see *The Nutcracker*. It was going to be a special Hogmanay holiday night out for us with Mum. Mum has changed a lot since the ballet school opened. A lot of the school's success rides on her shoulders because she is principal ballet teacher. I suppose I have felt that she has other things on her mind the whole time and, much as she tries to make more time for her own kids, it often doesn't work out. All the cosy moments we had in the cottage, along with the home baking, delicious soups and home-made gifts, are a thing of the past. And I don't know how poor little Sorcha and Hamish feel about it, because when I was their age Mum was a full-time mother. Now she is anything but. In fact, Mum has been as stressed as I've ever seen her.

Not only did it hurt my feelings that she was cross and impatient at times, I also felt an idiot for putting her in that situation by wanting to have my own ballet school. And, let's be honest, something I stupidly had not thought about beforehand, was that I get very jealous when she admires other dancers. Leo is an amazing dancer, as well as being quite difficult to get along with, and she caused a few arguments between me and Mum. We sorted that out last term but now Mum has told me that another new girl is coming to join us this term – Velvet Hughes. It's a strange time of year for a new student to arrive and I'm worried about how that will unbalance things. I just want everything to settle down the way it is. Anyway, I also know that Mum's still an amazing mother and she's always thinking about the family, as well as everything else she has to do – that's why she had the idea of our trip to see the Scottish Ballet.

Dad and Hamish said they'd had enough of ballet to last them a lifetime; they organised an evening of playing pool on Hamish's brand new table, which Hamish was just as excited about as we were about the ballet. It was the highlight of our holidays. I just couldn't wait!

Of course it was lovely to see the grannies and grandpas at Christmas. They travelled up to visit, all laden with beautiful gifts and hampers of yummy food. But I missed ballet, and as there were no ballet classes in the holidays, going to see the Scottish Ballet was the most exciting thing in the calendar. We were due to go on January 10, just three days before the rest of the ballet students would return to us for second term. I suppose I knew that this would be the last time for a while that Sorcha and I would have Mum all to ourselves, which was another reason why it was a *very* special event.

After Hogmanay, when the grannies and grandpas went home, it seemed like time stretched on forever, but the 10th finally came around and Sorcha and I lay on my bed chatting in our pyjamas, even though it was about two o'clock in the day. Much as we try to stick to a proper routine at Christmas, we just never can.

"What are we going to wear to the ballet tonight, Katie?" she asked.

"I dunno. What do you want to wear?" I said.

"One of the new dresses I got for Christmas," she said decisively.

"Let me see what I've got." I jumped up and slung open the doors of my wardrobe. "Hmm, what would look good?"

"Something pretty as it's such a pretty ballet, Katie."

Sorcha had always loved *The Nutcracker* but had learned more about it while we made the tree decorations and now she was completely obsessed with it. Ballet and sweeties were her two favourite things in the world – put them together and she had found her perfect treat!

I took out a white lace top and black leggings and held them up in front of the mirror.

"These would look smart together, don't you think?" I said.

"Aren't you going to wear a dress?" Sorcha sounded really shocked. "What would Clara think of leggings?"

I laughed. Sorcha loves dresses, and she likes it when I wear them too.

We've been to the theatre to watch ballet a few times with Mum, and I suppose it's true that I always *have* worn dresses in the past. In fact, Sorcha and I often wear similar things when we go out for special occasions. Part of me feels I'm getting too old for dressing like my little sister, but I don't want to let her down. I mean, it's not as if Tilda or Catriona are going to see what I'm wearing and discuss our styles, like they usually do.

"Well, you tell me what you're thinking of wearing, and I will try to fit in with you," I said.

"I'm planning to wear my new purple dress, the corded one," announced Sorcha. "With a crossover ballet cardigan in lilac. Could you wear something purple too?"

"But Sorch, surely we can wear different colours now," I said gently.

She looked so sad, that I decided to wear a cosy lilac jersey mini-dress, with toasty purple tights and brown suede boots. I tried it all on.

"There, how does that look to my personal stylist?"

"Very good. I approve," she said. "And we have to wear our hair in buns."

"Okay, buns it is, Fairy Bossy-Boots!" I laughed, throwing one of my pillows at her.

"I'll get my dress on first so I don't mess the bun up with it!" She ran off to get changed.

Sorcha and I were ready way before Mum and we paced around impatiently, then twirled down the hall, dancing like the Sugar Plum Fairy. When Mum finally came to tell us it was time to leave, she looked absolutely lovely. She had chosen her knee-length black velvet dress with long black boots. Her hair was pinned up loosely and she wore a little of her really pale frosted lipstick.

"Can we wear some lipstick and perfume too?" asked Sorcha.

"Yes, of course," said Mum. "Sit by the light and I'll do your lips."

"Do you think we'll see Willow at the ballet, Mummy?" asked Sorcha, as Mum applied some lipstick.

We both love Mum's teaching assistant, Willow, who is a professional dancer with the Scottish Ballet but is helping us out for a few months at Cloudberry.

"I don't think so sweetie, she's on a little holiday before term starts again here," explained Mum.

"I'd love to see Willow dance on the stage," said Sorcha.

"Same here," I said, pursing my lips for mum as she applied the frosted pink lipstick, which she said was called "Sugar Plum".

4. Thoughts of Mallie

We said goodbye to Dad and Hamish, who were obviously dying to get rid of us so they could begin their pool contest. Hamish revealed that he and Dad had bought lots of jelly sweets in the village shop that afternoon – something Mum doesn't always approve of, as she says jelly sweets are the very worst thing for sitting in your teeth and causing cavities.

"Have a great time!" called Dad, as we jumped in the car for the hour-and-a-half drive down to Edinburgh. "And remember, Katie, one day we'll be driving to watch you perform in a big ballet like that!"

"That's a long way off, Dad," I said. "But thanks anyway for your faith in me!"

"Right, away you go. And have fun!" said Dad.

"We know when we're not wanted!" joked Mum, blowing kisses to Dad.

As we set off down the drive of the Cloudberry estate with the scent of Mum's Diorissimo perfume filling the car from every seat, I turned back to look up at Cloudberry Castle. A few flakes of snow fell and it looked so beautiful against the twilight sky, with lights glowing at the windows of our flat on the first floor. The four turrets look so intriguing and the central clock tower, which always reads two o'clock, stands proudly in the middle. Even though the castle has caused us such a lot of hard work and stress, along with the fact that I had been scared of a ghost in the old nursery in there for a while, I still couldn't think of any better place to live.

Mum and Sorcha chatted across the seats about the plot of *The Nutcracker*.

"Tell me the celebration dances again," said Sorcha. "You know, the ones organised by the Sugar Plum Fairy."

"Well," said Mum, "there's the chocolate dance, the tea and coffee dances, the marzipan dance, Mother Ginger's dance and of course the wonderful Waltz of the Flowers."

"Oh, that's *lovely*," said Sorcha. "It's led by the Dewdrop Fairy."

"Well done!" said Mum.

I smiled. Sorcha was so sweet and such a little sponge, soaking up everything she heard. As they chattered on, I got lost in my thoughts. There was this weird tugging feeling at the bottom of my tummy. I'd had it for a while, but hadn't really faced up to what was causing it. The car sped along the country roads leading to the Forth Road Bridge, and a light flurry of snow fell on the windows.

The problem felt very clear all of a sudden. It was Mallie, my old best friend. It was January 10 now, the Christmas and New Year holiday was almost over, and I still hadn't heard from her.

Once, she and I did ballet classes together in the village. Mrs Miller, our first ballet teacher, moved away to Australia because of her husband's job. I think that was what really inspired Mum to start the ballet school: she wasn't happy with the idea that I might not find other ballet lessons locally. I loved dancing with Mallie, but now that I was caught up with the school the whole time, I was worried that we'd never do that again. I'd gained so much ballet, but by doing that, I'd lost Mallie. She and I always used to have the best laughs.

I had been hoping each day that my phone would ring and her number would show in the screen. But it had been three weeks of waiting, so I was starting to give up on the idea of hearing back from her.

I had thought she would love the card.

"Katie," said Mum from the front of the car. "We're nearly in Edinburgh."

"Sorry, I was miles away just now," I said.

"I know you were," laughed Mum. "I had to say your name three times!"

"Did you? Sorry. I was thinking about Mallie."

"Oh, Katie, I'm sorry you don't see Mallie these days. I haven't seen her mum in ages either. I used to see her at choir, but I can't fit that in anymore. And I hardly shop in the village because Mr Renton gets our food shop and Mrs Mathers makes such lovely meals in the school. So I don't seem to see our local friends at the moment."

"Never mind," I said. "Maybe one day."

"Yes, we can pick up the pieces, I'm sure," said Mum.

5. A Special Treat

By now, we were in George Street in the heart of Edinburgh; the Christmas lights were still strung across above us. I could see the castle up to the right, and the shops looked lovely and twinkly, as they still had Christmas decorations in their windows. We crossed onto the Bridges by the Balmoral Hotel and soon after that Mum started to look for a parking space. We found one fairly easily and went to an Italian restaurant for a quick meal. I put my sadness about Mallie to one side and let my thoughts be taken up by *The Nutcracker*. We had delicious spaghetti with a creamy sauce and garlic bread, but I could hardly swallow it because I was so excited about the ballet.

"Come on," said Mum. "Let's skip pudding

and get going. We can have ice cream during the interval."

As we approached the huge glass doors of the theatre, Mum turned to Sorcha and I with a wide smile on her face.

"I've actually got a little surprise for you two," she said. "Willow has managed to arrange a backstage tour for us! Come on. We just have to find a girl called Lara. She's going to take us to meet the Scottish Ballet dancers and to see what happens behind the scenes!"

"Yipppeee!" said Sorcha. "That's amazing!"

"Cool!" I said. "Thanks Mum. Ever since we saw *Swan Lake* at Covent Garden a couple of years ago, I've wondered what happens back stage at ballets!"

I couldn't wait to see the ballerinas! It was the best surprise imaginable.

We found Lara waiting inside at the Press Desk.

"Ah, the famous Mackenzies!" she said. "Come this way. We've heard so much about you."

Sorcha turned to me with a huge proud smile across her face.

"This is fun, Katie," she said. "Mum's just like she used to be!"

I squeezed her hand. Lovely little Sorcha. She

was very understanding about the changes the ballet school had brought to our lives, for a little girl.

Lara whisked us through a door that said

"Come this way," she said. "The dancers and the stage manager are looking forward to meeting you!"

"Wow!" said Sorcha. "Fantastic!"

The first thing I noticed was that the backstage area was a lot drabber and greyer looking than the theatre's front of house. There was no swirly gold paintwork, or red velvet seats, or painted cherubs. But that meant that the pretty ballerinas who floated around the backstage area looked even more stunning. Seriously, there were so many ballerinas! It was hard to know what to look at first, because there were so many delicious tutus on show. And there were loads of people dressed in black, too, who were organising lighting, sound and special effects. There must be so much to think about when you stage a huge ballet like this.

There was a scrumptious display of costumes hanging on a fancy rail – really, they made you crave sweeties, because there are so many types of yummy, sugary treats in *The Nutcracker*. The hanger of each outfit had a little note, naming the character and dancer it was for. Some dancers were still wearing joggers and cardigans, but had already had their buns and full make-up done. The make-up was great. A bit heavy for real life, but I'd love to get the chance to wear make-up like that on stage, with dark smoky eyeshadow and rose-pink blush and lips. So pretty, like Anna Pavlova.

"Oooh, look! I love the angel tutus!" cried Sorcha.

"So do I!" I agreed. "And see the dolls – Harlequin and Columbine – and the nasty Mouse King. And look at the Candy Cane performers!"

"Lara," said Sorcha, "how long does it take to make all the costumes?"

"Good question, Sorcha. There's a costume department at Scottish Ballet working just on costumes all year long!"

"Wow!"

"And it takes a while to collect and make all the props too. We order some things from e Bay," said Lara. "Now, if you look up high above the stage, you will see that the scenery drops down from a rail up there."

We craned our necks up and it looked like there

were eight or more layers of scenery, somehow suspended on high rails, so we knew that the stage was going to look beautiful throughout the show.

"And this here," said Lara, pointing to a huge noticeboard, "is the dancers' rota for the whole tour. As you can see, many of the dancers can perform several of the roles, and we swap around who will dance which part. This way it give them lots of experience and it means we don't have a problem if any one of the dancers gets ill or called away. This is where the dancers will check out what they're expected to dance for the evening."

"Gosh, that's amazing," I said. "They have so much to learn. I don't know how they remember all the different steps for each character!"

"Oh, I remember that when I was with the New York City Ballet," said Mum. "That's what it's like being a professional ballerina – it's a lot of hard work."

"Ah, you danced with the NYC troupe?" said Lara. "They are amazing."

"Yes," said Mum. "The standard is even higher now than when I joined. Actually, they're doing *The Nutcracker* this year at the Lincoln Centre in New York."

"Yes, I heard about that. I'm sure it will be lovely," said Lara. "New York is such a wonderful city."

I saw that one ballerina was having her feet strapped up with tape and bandages by a medical assistant, and they appeared to be very sore.

She saw us looking and smiled. "It's worth it, girls," she said. "When you're out there dancing across the stage, you don't feel the pain. You get carried along on a wave of energy. It's the best feeling in the world."

I was used to Mum telling me about her sore feet and aching limbs when she was in the New York City ballet, but it was amazing to see it all up close. It didn't put me off one bit; even though the dancers looked so feminine and fragile, they were really strong and powerful and could perform amazing feats.

"How would you like to meet this evening's Sugar Plum Fairy?" asked Lara.

"Definitely!" I beamed.

"Yes please! Where is she?" asked Sorcha, eyes darting around.

"She's in her dressing room," explained Lara. "And I happen to know that she's already dressed for the role, so we can visit her there."

Sorcha and I giggled with excitement. I had always wondered what it would be like inside a real ballerina's dressing room.

The name on the black door read:

MARIANNA
CAPPALDI

Willow had told me about this dancer. She said she was easily the most talented of her generation. My knees trembled as we went inside.

6. The Sugar Plum Fairy

There she sat in front of her reflection in the mirror – one of the mirrors you always expect to see in a dressing room, with lights all around it – and it was like seeing two perfect and identical Sugar Plum Fairies at once. The costume was gorgeous. The bodice was soft ivory satin, covered in pretty sparkles, while the skirt was softest pink, made from hundreds of separate layers of finest tulle. And the tiara was the best thing of all – it was a mixture of sparkling diamonds and pretty sugar plums. Mum had explained to me once that sugar plums are not in fact plums with sugar on them; it's the name of a pretty sweetie made from dried cherries and apricots, boiled into an oval shape. At one time, Mum said, plum was the word used for any sort of dried fruit.

Marianna was very tiny and pretty, and had her dark hair pulled into a perfect twist-knot.

"Hi girls," she said. "Lovely to see you. Are you excited about the show?"

"Yes," chimed Sorcha and I, taking in all the wonderful details of the dressing room, like the array of good luck cards on the walls, and the intriguing pots of make-up and moisturiser, plus the hair accessories basket, which was crammed full of kirby grips, hair nets, sparkly clasps and pretty combs.

"Would you like to try the tiara on?" asked Marianna.

"I'd love to," I said.

"Me too," whispered Sorcha, so thrilled that the words were barely audible.

We took turns sitting in Marianna's chair and she placed the tiara on our heads. Sorcha went first and looked adorable as her pink cheeks burned with pride. When Marianna lowered it onto my head, I gasped. As I stared into the mirror, I got lost in my dreams again and imagined that I was going out onto the stage to dance the part of the Sugar Plum Fairy. In fact it was even better than that: in my imagination I was *being* the Sugar Plum Fairy, ruling my Land of Sweets.

"I guess we should get you through to the auditorium now," said Lara.

"Oh, sorry," I said, coming out of my daydreams with a start. It was hard to take the tiara off, but I knew it was time to become a part of the audience. It's just that my heart lies in being part of the ballet troupe, and that's how I will always be.

"Goodbye, girls," said Marianna. "I hope you enjoy the show."

"We will," I said.

Lara took us back out into the red and gold public part of the theatre, which suddenly appeared very bright and fancy after being backstage – maybe too bright and fancy. I felt more connected to the world behind the scenes, where the performance is made and everything seems more real and less showy.

We settled into our seats, which were bang in the centre of the auditorium.

"Are we allowed any sweeties?" asked Sorcha.

"Well," said Mum. "Funny you should say that. As this is a Hogmanay treat, and as this is *The Nutcracker*..."

"And as Hamish and Dad have a *ton* of sweeties..." I added.

"Yes, I noticed that, I must admit," said Mum. "Anyway, as I was saying, because this is such a special occasion, I did get you some sweeties!"

"Hooray!" said Sorcha, taking a little box from mum full of pretty sweets called "Sugar Plums."

"I saw them in Perth before Christmas and I couldn't resist them," explained Mum.

They were super-delicious.

The orchestra struck up with *The Nutcracker* overture, the lights dimmed, the safety curtains swished to either side of the stage. The performance had begun!

Sorcha and I didn't budge except for getting ice cream at the interval. The gala party scene was lovely, and the mice were brilliantly horrid. The Land of Snow was sparkly and gorgeous. But it was the Land of Sweets that I loved most of all. I loved it when Marianna came on as the Sugar Plum Fairy. She danced the part beautifully. I watched every step she made: the coupés, développés and pas de chats. She had a brilliant way of doing the battement glissé too.

The audience stood at the end, giving the cast a standing ovation. Sorcha and I clapped until the palms of our hands itched.

I didn't want to leave the theatre and trade that fairy-tale magic for real life again, but Mum was anxious to see whether Hamish had overdosed on sweets, so we got back into the car and headed home towards Perth.

"I'd love to dance the part of the Sugar Plum Fairy," I said.

"Katie, you will," said Mum. "Have patience, darling."

"That was a brilliant treat, Mum," I said. "Thank you."

All the way home in the car, I imagined I was dancing the part of the Sugar Plum Fairy on a big international stage – a stage that was filled with lovely dolls and candy ballerinas – with an audience who applauded my performance until their palms itched. This was nothing but a ballet dream.

I was pleased I would be seeing all my lovely friends again soon at Cloudberry Castle. There was still that difficult feeling about Mallie. I didn't know whether it meant anything that she hadn't replied to my card. Perhaps it meant nothing, or perhaps we weren't friends anymore? The thought of dear old Mallie was so much more appealing than the idea of a new girl starting at Cloudberry, like this Velvet Hughes. Mum says she's coming from America, from Hollywood in fact. I wonder whether she's been living a more glamorous lifestyle than we can ever match? I just don't think she's going to fit in easily.

7. The New Term

The day after the performance of *The Nutcracker*, I went to the costume room in the castle and found the prettiest tutu I could. Ever since I first discovered the secret ballroom in Cloudberry, which is now our fabulous ballet studio, I have loved dancing round that elegant space. It's the best way to get things out of my mind.

The sweetie-pink tutu I found wasn't *quite* gorgeous enough for the Sugar Plum Fairy, so I took it up to my bedroom and looked in my box of sewing bits and pieces, where I keep pretty beads, bows and sequins. I added some frosted pink beads and sugar-pink ribbons. There! That was better now. I put on the tutu and stared at myself in front of the mirror. It made me tingle, as if I really was a fairy, not a normal girl.

I added a very sparkly tiara, and completed the outfit with a wand. I went downstairs after that, and found *The Nutcracker* music in Mum's collection. I wanted to spend some time on my own and fill my head with music and movement so there wouldn't be room for worries.

I put on the music for the dance of the Sugar Plum Fairy and tried to recall all the steps I'd seen Marianna do so beautifully in Edinburgh. *The Nutcracker* is especially magical when Clara arrives in the Land of Sweets, and I wanted more than anything to perfect this dance and make it mine.

I whirled around the studio, trying out the assemblé with battement glissé. After that, I danced the Waltz of the Flowers, acting as the Dewdrop Fairy. As usual, I felt completely happy as I danced. I only stopped when I eventually became completely exhausted.

Over the next couple of days, I took my clothes and jewellery back up to the room I shared in term time with Tilda and Catriona and arranged it all there. The room looked so plain and empty without all our girly stuff in it. I wanted it to be cosy and welcoming for them, so I pinned up a few posters and sorted out our DVD collection, and I added some accessories to the room, like little floral cushions I'd got from Granny Mackenzie for Christmas. I put some snowdrops in vases and, finally, I brought up my Sugar Plum tutu and hung it on a hook by my bed.

Mrs Mathers returned the next day, to whoops of delight from Hamish and Sorcha. Her jolly face around the school, as well as the comforting smell of her fairy cakes and breads, was lovely. The school teachers arrived, and lovely Willow came back too. It was January 14 when the smiley face of Tilda Forbes came racing up the stairs of the castle.

"Katie Mackenzie!" she cried, hugging me. "I missed you! Hey, I got a laptop for Christmas. And there's a ballet game on it. Help me unpack and we can play on it, and chat to ballerinas at other ballet schools. It will be loads of fun!"

"Brilliant, Tilda!" I said. "You look great!"

"Thanks. Do you like my boots? We got them in Aberdeen for £20, but they're not bad, are they?" she said.

"They're cool. I can't wait to hear all your news."

"Snap!" said Tilda.

I opened the door to our little sitting room, just off the bedroom we share with Millie.

"Ta-da!" I said.

"Oh, Katie, it looks really pretty. Oooh, I'm so happy to be back!" she said. "There was no fun at all at home. It's so dull compared with Cloudberry!"

"I know. It was crazy here last term, wasn't it? Hey, Tilda, what do you think this new girl, Velvet Hughes, will be like?" I asked.

"I don't know," said Tilda. "We'll have to wait until she gets here."

"Yeah, I just hope she doesn't change things," I said.

"I know, me too," Tilda agreed. "I like things here the way they are."

We heard wheels on the gravel and ran to look out of the window. It was a big chauffeur-driven car, followed by a large and familiar black trailer.

"Ah, there's Leo now. Followed by the Duke in his luxury horsebox. Let's go and welcome her," said Tilda.

We had sorted out our differences with Leo in the first term, but her mother was still a piece of work and, at her age, I didn't think that would ever change.

By the time Tilda and I got down to the landing above reception, Leo's mother, Mrs McLennan, was already getting onto Mum about this and that. We hovered on the landing, listening.

"I've been thinking about the provision you made

last term for Leo's allergies... I'd like to see a bit more variety this year," she said.

"We'll see what Mrs Mathers can do," said Mum. "But to be honest with you, Mrs McLennan, I think we did a very good job for Leo. She never felt hungry, I don't think. And if you don't like our provision, then perhaps another ballet school could accommodate her needs better?"

Tilda and I looked at each other and smiled.

"Your Mum is catching on. Nice one!" whispered Tilda. "Someone has to stand up to that stupid woman."

Mrs McLennan was speechless for a moment.

"Well, I mean, I suppose if you stick to what you did before, that would be fine," she said.

Mum caught sight of us on the landing. She winked.

But Mrs McLennan continued.

"And if there are any opportunities for Leo to audition for a professional ballet performance, then I'd like to be notified immediately. I'd like to see her on the stage commercially before the year is out."

"Mrs McLennan, our girls are far too young for us to be thinking of them as earning ballerinas. However, if anything appropriate comes up, I'll let you know.

Now, I really must be getting on with things," snapped Mum.

Tilda and I ran down the last part of the stairs towards the reception area.

"Hey Leo!" I called.

"Katie! Tilda! I really missed you," she said, embracing us.

"We've missed you too! And the Duke!" I said.

"Let's go and see if he's settling in," she suggested.

"Sure. Let's do that!" I replied. "Okay, Tilda?"

"Yeah, sure."

Leo was definitely a proper friend now, so maybe the new girl, Velvet, would become one too.

8. Velvet Hughes

That day was really hectic with everyone arriving back. Once we'd checked on the Duke and taken some of Leo's things upstairs for her, Tilda and I saw Catriona coming up the drive, so we went to welcome her.

"Hey Catriona, great to see you!" I said.

But she was distracted. She was staring at one of the dads who were standing around in reception. She pointed at him secretly and mouthed: "Is he famous?"

Tilda and I stared at him curiously. He had long brown hair and wore very scruffy jeans with a faded leather jacket. He didn't seem like any of the other dads who were there to drop off girls. He looked as if he didn't have a regular job, like maybe he was an artist or something.

"Hey, I've seen him somewhere before," said Tilda.

"He's definitely famous!" whispered Catriona.

"Yeah. Very familiar," I agreed.

"This might sound crazy," said Tilda, "but isn't he in a film that came out recently?"

"Yes, that's it!" I said. "It's Johnny Hughes, from the *Mermaid* films. He's King Neptune, isn't he?"

"I – do – not – believe – it!" said Tilda. "It *is* King Neptune! Awesome! The *Mermaid* films are my favourites."

"Wait a minute!" I said. "Johnny *Hughes*. He must be Velvet's dad!"

"Incredible!" said Tilda. "We're going to have the daughter of *the* Johnny Hughes here at Cloudberry? I can't believe it. She must know loads of movie stars through her dad. This is all *so* meant to be. Because I've always wanted to live in Hollywood! My Granny Forbes says I'm a natural star! You know, I think we do need new blood here. I'm sure Velvet will fit in. I'll help her."

I stared at Tilda. "Didn't you say you weren't keen on change?"

"Did I?" said Tilda, looking around reception for Velvet. "Ah, that must be her! Let's go and say 'hi.' Katie, we've got to give everyone a chance."

Tilda made a beeline for Velvet while I stood open-mouthed at her turnaround.

Velvet *did* look very cool and pretty, I must admit. She wore a skater dress with long sleeves and a short full skirt in a really lovely shade of cerise pink. It was the sort of dress that made you wish that was exactly what you were wearing at that moment. Velvet had really long, straightened blonde hair, which was a soft ash colour, and I'm sure she wore one stroke of eyeliner across her eyelids, but it was so cleverly applied you could hardly see it.

"Oh, hi. You must be Velvet?" said Tilda. "Welcome to Cloudberry."

"Oh, thanks," said Velvet with a broad smile, showing dazzlingly white teeth. "Is it always this cold here? I'm used to a lot more sunshine in L.A."

"You'll get used to it," said Tilda. "But the castle could do with a bit more heating, it's true."

I stared at Tilda. I was a bit hurt by that comment – there she was, using a complaint against the ballet school to get chummy with a brand new girl, who we really didn't know anything about.

Velvet's phone rang.

"That's Patsy Parker's new song, isn't it?" said Tilda, noticing the ringtone. "I love it."

"Oh, thanks," said Velvet. "She's a good friend of mine."

"No way! You know Patsy Parker?" Tilda eyes were stretched wide with excitement.

"Yeah, it's no big deal," said Velvet.

Before I knew it, Tilda had made her way over to Velvet's dad. It seemed that Velvet was introducing Tilda.

"Oh, I love all your work," I could hear Tilda gushing. "How do you film the underwater world in the *Mermaid* movies?"

"Ah, it's a secret." Velvet's dad sounded polite but a little abrupt.

Tilda was not put off. "Can I have your autograph?" she asked.

"Well, I don't usually do stuff like that when I'm dealing with Velvet's education, but I'll make an exception this one time!"

Tilda was a fast mover. She dashed off to get paper and pen, and then began to tell him what he should write.

"If you just put: 'To Tilda...'" she began.

"It's okay, I kind of know what to put," said Johnny Hughes.

"So you live in Hollywood?" Tilda continued.

"We have a house there," said Johnny Hughes. "But we also have a place in London."

"Cool," said Tilda. "London's fun too."

Mum came rushing over to deal with Johnny Hughes, perhaps realising that Tilda was getting carried away. Tilda immersed herself in a deep discussion with Velvet after that, so I fiddled with some brochures near reception.

I was intrigued by the conversation between Mum and Velvet's dad.

"So, you think you can get her movie-ready?" asked Johnny Hughes.

"I think so. She has *some* natural ability," said Mum. "And she *looks* like a talented ballerina, and holds herself as such, which is very important."

"Sure, I mean they can use a real dancer for the trickier scenes, but they want her to have a genuine feel for it," said Johnny. "I really appreciate you taking her for just a term. She's always wanted to be in a film, and this one is a perfect fit."

"Yes, it sounds great. What did you say the title will be?"

"*Sugar Plum*," said Johnny. "I've put in a lot of funding. I mean it's about time there was a ballet movie for the kids who love to dance, rather than an adult take on it."

"I quite agree," said Mum. "It should be a hit.

And we'll do all we can to prepare her."

So, Velvet Hughes not only had a film-star dad, she was going to be a star herself! And she'd only come here to Cloudberry to learn to dance for her role – in a ballet movie called *Sugar Plum*. Mum was going to have to turn her into an expert dancer in a few weeks.

Great: here was another girl who would try to get everything her own way. And imagine starring in a movie about the Sugar Plum Fairy when you don't even care about ballet! It's so not fair. I've never even performed the Sugar Plum yet, and I've been training in ballet most of my life.

I turned round to speak to Tilda, but I saw her back disappearing upstairs with Velvet. Tilda was carrying Velvet's backpack, and looking up at her with puppy-dog eyes.

"So, tell me all about Patsy Parker," she was saying.

Later on that evening I started to feel bad about not wanting Velvet here. I knew I ought to at least give her a chance. I was going past her door, so I popped my head around to say goodnight. She didn't expect me, and was checking out a website about Patsy Parker, and taking notes! She didn't realise I'd seen, and I didn't say a word.

Over the next few days, I hardly saw Tilda. She

and Velvet Hughes became best friends, and Catriona and I hung out together more.

"She's just gotten carried away," Catriona said about Tilda. "Because she's really into Hollywood."

"I know. I don't blame her," I said. "It's just a bit of a turnaround from what she was first saying."

"Exactly!" agreed Catriona.

First I lost Mallie and now it seemed like Tilda had moved on to a new friend already. I came to realise that no matter what you have to impress your friends with, such as your very own ballet school, there's always someone who comes along with something that appears even better. And really, you shouldn't need to impress true friends with anything except your company, should you?

I told myself that it would probably only take a few days for Tilda to stop worshipping Velvet, but the way that she chattered on in our room at night was unbearable.

"Velvet has lunch at the Beverley Hills Wilshire Hotel the whole time," said Tilda. "And she says I can go when I'm out there. The Hugheses have a regular table and we'll get the best service, obviously."

"You mean you're going out to Los Angeles?" asked Catriona.

"Of course I am," said Tilda. "In the summer.

And we're going to Malibu Beach, and we're sure to see loads of film stars when we go out for dinner every night. That's what Velvet says will happen. And when she's filming the big ballet movie, *Sugar Plum*, I'll go on set and everything."

I sighed. I didn't know whether to feel angry, jealous or just sad. I was sure Tilda was deceived somehow in her adoration of Velvet, but she'd have to work that out for herself.

"Are you okay, Katie?" asked Tilda.

"Yeah, I'm fine."

"Oh, that's good," said Tilda. "Because I'm having the best time ever at Cloudberry this term. Did you know that Velvet has her own publicist – that's a person who tells newspapers and TV what to write about you. Velvet's publicist is called Paloma and she says that Velvet'll have such a lot of interviews when *Sugar Plum* comes out. I'll probably have to go with her, to fix her hair and stuff."

It was as if Tilda had been brainwashed.

9. Mallie Lennox

The best thing about the new term starting was that Willow's lovely ballet lessons began again. It was nice to be taught by a gorgeous young dancer like Willow. She was so pretty, with dark glossy hair, wide violet eyes and pink rosebud lips.

"Girls, we have a really hard term ahead," she explained, "as we are preparing for exams just before the Easter break."

"Who will examine us?" asked Leo.

"I'm just coming to that. The Royal Academy of Dance will send their head examiner, Mrs Jennifer Capers, and she will award you Grade Five RAD – *if* you dance to her satisfaction. I have here the sheet that explains what we will cover for Grade Five. Please take one and pass it on."

I studied the sheet when I received my copy. There looked like such a lot to perfect:

Grand Allegro

Pirouette

Balancé

Changement adage

Battement tendu

Rond de jambe

Port de bras

Glissade

Sauté

Soubresaut

Free Dance – The candidate should prepare a short expressive dance of their own choice.

"I don't have to learn all this," whispered Velvet to Tilda. "I just have to get ready for the movie."

"You're lucky. I'll have to take the exam," said Tilda. "Unless I can get a part in the film too?"

"I'll ask Dad," said Velvet. "I mean, he's in charge of it, so it should be fine."

I turned away and chatted through the exam sheet with Catriona, Eliza and Polly. Even though I was feeling a bit lonely, I was determined to really excel in my ballet this term. But it would have been lovely to practice with the old Tilda. My aim was to get a distinction in the RAD exam – at least it was something to focus on.

I hardly went into Lochvale village now that I didn't go to school there. But one Saturday during February, I decided to go down to the village with Catriona to get some shampoo and stuff like that. While we were browsing around the pharmacy, looking at nail polish, I heard a familiar voice on the other side of the shop. When I looked up, I spotted Mallie at the counter.

"Do you have antiseptic cream?" she was asking the pharmacist. "I'm covered in bumps, cuts and bruises."

"Yes, sure," said the pharmacist. "You've been in the wars?"

"Och, my new horse keeps bucking me off!" she said. "He must be trying to tell me something!"

I just had to talk to Mallie. I moved towards

her; she noticed me and smiled nervously, in the way you do when you're not quite sure if you're still okay with someone.

"Hey, Mallie!" I said. "Nice to see you!"

"Katie, you too!" she said, coming towards me.

We hugged each other uncertainly. "Oh, this is Catriona," I said. "She's a boarder at Cloudberry."

"Hi Catriona," said Mallie. "How are you enjoying it?"

"Hey Mallie," said Catriona. "It's fun being at ballet school, but we've got exams this term."

"Oh, drats!" said Mallie, with a smile. "I hate exams."

"So, Mal, you seem to be a bit bruised?" I said.

"Oh, don't ask. I've got a pony that I absolutely adore, but he's had a bad time, and he's really panicky. He keeps chucking me – I've lost count of how often I've come off him," giggled Mallie.

"Oh dear! Sounds a bit more feisty than our little Bella. I saw him in your stable when I popped round – he's adorable."

"Yes, one of Dad's friends was feeding him while we were away. We just got back yesterday – which reminds me, thanks for the lovely card. It's so pretty!"

"I'm glad you like it," I said. "You've had a long

trip away, but now I see you it seems like just yesterday that we were last together."

"Exactly," agreed Mallie. "Did you notice that Mickey's really anxious?"

"Yeah, poor boy. He was terrified when I approached him. I could see the whites of his eyes."

"Yeah, he does that. As I said, he's been badly treated in the past and he needs lots of tender loving care to bring him along. Dad got him from a friend who simply went along to his previous owner with a horsebox and said: 'Either I take the pony, or I report you to the RSPCA, which is it?' Apparently, the man used to smack him across the face the whole time. And that's why he cowers when you go near him: he thinks he's going to get smacked again," said Mallie. "He very sensitive about his head."

"Oh, that's such a shame. How could anyone be cruel to such a lovely horse?" I said. "Or any horse, for that matter?"

"Exactly and once you get to know him, he's a sweetheart – a really lovely horse, it's just that he needs lots of time spent with him," said Mallie. "And I can't seem to do enough! Half the time I'm in too much pain from my tumbles!"

"Is anyone else working with him too?" I asked.

"No, it's really all down to me. Rory and Finn are hopeless. They never want to help."

"Well," I said, "if you ever need some help with him, I'd *love* to come over. I mean Bella is my favourite horse in the whole world, but she's really the estate's horse, and she's too small for me to ride now. And there's this girl called Leo who's at Cloudberry now, who has a pony called the Duke, and she's kind of taken over the stables with all her stuff, so I don't enjoy it there as much anymore."

"Do you really mean it, Katie?" Mallie looked relieved and very pleased. "You would come and help? That would be fantastic, because it would break my heart to give up on him. Could you come over on Saturday afternoon, and see how he responds to you?"

"Yeah, sure, that's perfect," I said. "I'll cycle over. And it means we can hang out again anyway!"

"Great! See you Saturday!" said Mallie. "Byyee!"

"Bye, Mallie."

Catriona and I headed back to the castle after that.

"She seems really nice," said Catriona.

"Oh, she is, she's just lovely!"

I wanted to skip and do cartwheels! Hooray! Mallie and I were friends again. And I was going to

59

get the chance to work on that lovely thoroughbred pony, Mickey. I couldn't wait.

Tilda might have got carried away with Velvet Hughes, but at least I had one of my special friends back.

10. A Lesson with Mum

On the Monday morning after that, Mum came to say she was going to take us for the daily ballet lesson. I always felt so proud of her when she was in teacher mode. Today she looked lovely in pale-pink ballet tights and shoes, a black leotard with a short black practice skirt over it, as well as a pale-pink crossover cardigan. Her hair was in a bun and she wore her sugar-plum-pink lipstick. Under her arm she carried her laptop computer, which she didn't usually bring to class, and she also had our video camera with her, which was even more strange. I wondered what she was going to do with it.

Much as Willow was the favourite teacher in the whole school, we all loved it when Mum taught us instead of Willow, because it was just an occasional treat and she always did fun stuff with us. Sometimes we would do improvisation, when we would act out animal movements or pretend to be trees.

But this time, she began by telling us that she'd be giving a lesson on the history of ballet.

There were groans all round. We love to dance and move about more than anything!

She gave us a little lecture and wrote notes on a big white board.

"Ballet," she began, "was invented in Italy in the fifteenth century. It was later further developed by the Russians and the French, who invented the short white tutu..."

Catriona put her hand up.

"Yes, Catriona?" said Mum.

"Excuse me, Mrs Mackenzie, I was just wondering why you've brought your laptop and camera today," said Catriona.

"Nice try at an interruption, Catriona, and I might have fallen for it, had I not three cunning children of my own," said Mum, with a laugh.

"Sorry," said Catriona. "It's just that we love doing exciting ballet stuff with you!"

"Well, let me get onto the part of the lesson that needs the computer and the camera. Have some patience," said Mum. "Now, firstly, can any of you name a famous ballerina?"

"Darcey Bussell!" said Polly.

"Yes, one of the very finest dancers of our generation," said Mum, writing the name on the board. "Her Princess Rose in the *Prince of the Pagodas* was completely perfect."

"Anna Pavlova!" said Eliza.

"Yes, she was a very dainty Russian dancer," said Mum. "She started the trend for tiny ballerinas."

"And the meringue pudding is named after her," added Eliza knowledgably.

"Yes, that's right. Any others?"

"Margot Fonteyn," I said.

"Yes, Margot Fonteyn was an exquisite dancer, who was wonderful in all her roles. Which roles do you think prima ballerinas always love to dance?" asked Mum.

"Coppelia," said Annie.

"Giselle," said Jennifer.

"The Swan Princess, Odine" said Allie.

"The Sugar Plum Fairy," I said.

"Good suggestions," said Mum. "All wonderful parts. But today, I want to talk to you about the Sugar Plum Fairy in particular, for a very special reason."

I could tell from her face that she was excited. "You see, girls, I have some rather interesting news for you," she said. "Come and gather round me in a circle."

We all sat cross-legged in the circle as Mum plugged in her computer and projected a website onto a big white screen.

"I'm going to show you a stunning clip of New York City Ballet on YouTube. It's a production of *The Nutcracker Suite,* which they performed five years ago at Christmas time in the Lincoln Centre in New York," explained Mum. "And I'm showing it to you for a very special reason, which I will explain later."

The overture from *The Nutcracker* began. We sat enthralled, watching the fabulous standard of the dancers and the delicate steps they performed as they acted out the movements of the dolls. The costumes and sets were fantastic and it took me back to the show I'd seen in the holidays in Edinburgh.

"Watch out for this beautiful battement fondu," said Mum. "Do you see how perfectly straight she keeps her legs?"

We nodded, following every step.

"And here is a rond de jambe en l'air," said Mum. "See the flicking of the leg from below the knee?"

We nodded.

It was fun to watch the ballet on the big screen and learn from such talented ballerinas. We sighed when it came to an end.

"The reason I've showed this to you today, girls," said Mum, "is that I have received a very interesting email from the New York City Ballet."

11. An Opportunity

We all sat up straight at once at this announcement.

"As some of you may know, New York City Ballet are performing *The Nutcracker Suite* at the Theatre Royal in London next Christmas," said Mum. "And they have an outreach programme for developing junior associates all round the world. It's a way for them to invest in future talent. They are looking for a British-based girl to play Clara for three special matinée performances in London!"

We all gasped as it dawned on us that such an opportunity might be opened to ballet school students.

A huge smile spread over Mum's face.

"They have asked me to send a clip of each of you dancing. Based on these clips, there is a chance that you will be invited to New York for a final audition, where you will meet the rest of the ballet company, as well as their Director of Ballet. They have asked the girls selected for audition to prepare a small section of Clara's dance. I would love it if some girls from Cloudberry were selected for audition! We could have such fun working on an audition piece."

"Wow!" we chorused.

"Oh, I so want to be in *The Nutcracker*," I whispered to myself.

It was one of my dearest dancing dreams, as I loved the ballet so much. I was very excited by the idea of going to audition in New York. Just imagine dancing as Clara for the New York City Ballet!

There was a buzz of excitement in the room.

"You would dance in front of audiences of twelve hundred people over the three performances. It would be exhausting, but the chance of a lifetime," said Mum.

I looked around and saw that Velvet Hughes seemed a bit miffed – perhaps she felt left out, because she's not a serious dance student. Leo looked very determined, and Polly seemed to draw herself up tall too. Anyone but Velvet would be fine as far as I was concerned. I mean, it takes years of hard work to develop the sorts of skills the girls at Cloudberry have.

And when you have to dance with true confidence and honesty, it shows. I really hoped one of us would be picked as Clara. That would show Velvet.

But Mum had more to say.

"And the reason I've brought the video camera is that I'm going to film each of you today, and send your clips, so that the Director of Ballet in New York can see if any of you are what they are looking for!"

"But what shall we dance, Mrs Mackenzie?" asked Allie.

"I am going to play a mixture of classical ballet music, and I want each of you to express yourself in ballet to that music," said Mum. "Try to forget I am filming. They are looking for natural movement and expressive talent. They will teach you the rest. Just get involved with the pieces of music and imagine what story they might be telling."

Everyone was super-excited and full of chatter.

"You'll be brilliant, Velvet," said Tilda.

"Thanks Tilda," said Velvet.

"Leo is easily the best dancer here," I said. "And Polly is wonderful too!"

"That's enough, girls," said Mum. "We'll let the ballet company decide who's most suited to their needs, shall we?"

"Sorry!" I said. I knew I had to learn to hold my tongue where Velvet was concerned, but she was so annoying, and Tilda made it ten times worse by always pandering to her.

Mum played an assortment of lovely music, from *Cinderella*, *Sleeping Beauty* and *Coppelia*, and talked us through a warm-up of stretches and gentle moves. I did not seriously consider the possibility of going to New York as there were so many brilliant dancers in the room, especially Leo, and of course I knew there were dancers working hard in ballet schools all over the country, so I just danced as if I was doing one of my private practice sessions in the studio in the holidays.

As I was doing a series of pirouettes across the floor, Velvet bumped into me and sent me flying across the studio.

"Whoops, sorry!" she trilled.

I bit my lip, even though I was sure she had done it on purpose to make me look clumsy on the film footage. Luckily Mum stepped in to save me.

"Oh, I can edit that bit out. Just an unfortunate collision. But even so, Velvet, you must show restraint or you might start to look a bit on the clumsy side."

Velvet's face went purple with rage. She hated it when things backfired on her, as she liked to be the one in control. Mum's ticking off must have unsettled her, as the next thing we knew, she tried a plié but got stuck and fell flat on her bottom.

"Are you going to edit that out, Madame Mackenzie?" she asked.

"Yes, I will," said Mum. "But we also need some footage of steps which do work well. So, keep trying!"

Catriona and I exchanged a smile. That seemed like Mum's way of saying that nothing Velvet had done on film was good enough yet.

We all carried on dancing our hearts out, and Mum kept the music rolling as some lovely steps were coming out of the improvisation.

Finally, she felt she had enough footage of everyone.

"Thanks, girls. Wind down and rest now," she said.

"That was fun," said Polly.

I hoped that Polly and Leo would be picked, as Polly was so sweet and Leo so talented. When I thought of the possibility of Velvet being selected, I felt cold and clammy. It would be unbearable if she got to audition.

12. An Offer from Mallie

I went down to our family flat after tea that night to have a chat with Mum.

"Hi Katie!" said Sorcha.

"Hi, sweetie," I said. "Where's Mum?"

"She's having a shower."

"Oh. What did you have for tea?"

"We've had lasagne, made by Dad!" said Sorcha. "It was lovely! Mum and Dad are nearly back to how they used to be!"

"Great!" I said. And it *was* great news, because when the ballet school first opened, Mum and Dad had been flat out busy, and I felt so guilty that my passion for ballet had affected Sorcha and Hamish.

Mum soon appeared, with a towel wrapped round her head, wearing her towelling robe.

"Katie, darling!" she said. "It's lovely to see you!"

"Yeah, I thought I'd pay you a visit," I said.

"Sure, something on your mind?"

"Just wondering how you thought the little audition thing went today?" I asked casually.

"Well, lots of lovely footwork," said Mum.

"Yes. And?"

"Expression was delightful. I think they'll be impressed with a few girls."

"Oh, that's good," I said.

"Yes, and you did beautifully Katie. Obviously, it's not for me to say, but you did stand out. So, let's just see what happens, shall we?"

"Yes. What did you think of Velvet?" I asked.

"Velvet's aims at this school are different to yours," said Mum. "Tilda would be unwise to copy her."

"Yeah, and Tilda's a lovely dancer too," I said.

"That's right. She is," agreed Mum.

"Well, I had better go and see what's happening with the girls."

"Okay, sweetheart. See you later," said Mum.

I kissed her on the cheek and ran back upstairs to chat to Catriona.

The week after I bumped into Mallie went by in a flash. There were exam classes, Mum's new ballet history lessons, and lots of other schoolwork too. Tilda and I still chatted and had fun together, but she was very much Velvet's best friend now, and that had changed her. I accepted that, but missed the friendship we'd shared in the first term. I really liked hanging out with Catriona, and I found that she was the same every day, never up or down. I hung out with Leo a lot of the time too, and although she was never going to be easy, we had an understanding of each other. Allie and Jennifer were now best friends, and Eliza and Millie got on really well but otherwise it was such a small school that we could all just hang out with whoever happened to be around.

On the Friday night, I went down to my own bedroom in the flat, and it was fun to look out my jodhpurs and riding boots, as well as my black velvet hard hat. I couldn't wait to go over to Mallie's farm the next morning. As well as seeing Mallie, I would be seeing Mickey and getting to know him.

Next morning, Sorcha came to sit on my bed while I got dressed.

"Which horse are you riding?" she asked.

"Well, I might not be riding him as such just yet, but its Mallie's new horse, Mickey."

"Oh, why can't you ride him yet?"

"Because he's very scared of people, as his previous owner didn't treat him well," I said.

"Mum's got a book called *The Horse Whisperer*," said Sorcha, "and she says it's about a cowboy who can make horses happy and confident when they get sad. Are you going to whisper to Mickey?"

"Well, I'm certainly not going to shout at him," I said.

I went to tell Mum that I was heading off to Mallie's.

"Oh, how lovely," said Mum. "I hope you have a super time, darling."

Just as I was getting ready to leave, I got a text from Mallie. It was the first time in ages that something had come in from her on my phone, and it was great to receive it.

Want 2 stay over 2nite? Will b fun. Rory n Finn r staying @ G'pa's, so they won't be bugging us. Cud have a midnite feast like the old times. C u soon xx

"Mum, can I stay over at the farm tonight?" I asked. "Mallie's just offered."

"Yes, of course, if that's okay with her mum. I think that would be great," said Mum. "I've noticed that Tilda and Velvet are inseparable at the moment."

"Yeah, but I know Tilda will see through her soon. I mean, I can't compete with the offer of lunches at the Beverley Wilshire Hotel and shopping trips on Sunset Boulevard..."

"Velvet's not here long. And *her* worry is that she has to pass herself off as a great dancer after only a term of teaching," said Mum.

I grabbed an overnight bag, said goodbye to Dad and Sorcha, and ran down the stairs to the kitchen.

"Mrs Mathers, have you got any goodies I could take to my old friend's house?"

"Of course I do, love," she said.

She gave me a lovely big cake box, covered in pink rosebuds, and filled with slices of chocolate cake, lemon drizzle cake and buttery flapjacks.

"Oooh, yummy. Thank you, Mrs Mathers!" I said.

"What are you going to be doing at your friend's house, love?" asked Mrs Mathers.

"I'm going to help tame her pony!"

"Tame him, eh?" said Mrs Mathers. "What's wrong with him?"

"Oh, he's very wild, as he's been mistreated."

"Well, you just be careful, sweetheart. We don't want any broken legs, or collarbones, do we? What if you hear that they want you to audition in New York, and you've got an injury? How would that be?"

"I'll be very careful, Mrs Mathers, I promise!" I put the cake box into my backpack, which I slipped on my back.

I dashed out to the courtyard, where we kept our bikes. Hamish was out there on his, cycling round little traffic cones, quite expertly.

"Nice control, Hamish," I said.

"Thanks, sis," he said. "Where you going?"

"To Mallie's."

"Aw, you hardly ever play with Sorcha and me anymore," he said. "I'd like to play hide-and-seek with you, like we used to."

"Alright Hamish, tomorrow when I get back, I promise that the three of us will play hide-and-seek in the grounds, okay?" I said.

"COOL!" He attempted to pull his front wheel up in a wheelie.

I jumped on my bike and began to pedal as fast as

I could. It was a great feeling, cycling over to Tullyacre with the wind in my hair. Wow! A night with Mallie *and* time at the farmhouse, which I hadn't had for ages, *and* I was going to ride with Mickey too!

13. Mallie's Cosy Farmhouse

The farmyard at Tullyacre looked just as messy as ever.

Rory and Finn were out in one of the sheds as I arrived.

"Hey, Katie," called Finn. "You wanna see our flying machine?"

"Yeah, I suppose so," I said, jumping off my bike and dashing across to the shed.

I saw some bits of old tractor lying in pieces. A few sections were tied together with rope and the boys were making wing shapes from an old wooden door.

"Well, what do you think?" asked Rory.

"Looks great," I said. "So long as I don't have to test it."

"What you trying to say, Katie Mackenzie?" said Finn. "Think it's rubbish? Think we can't fly to Glasgow in this? Is that what you're saying?"

I giggled, and Rory turned to come after me.

I flew round the yard with Finn and Rory chasing.

"We'll dunk your head in the cow's manure pile," said Rory.

"Aaargghh!" I cried. "Please don't do that. I do believe you can fly to Glasgow in it, honestly I do!"

At that moment, Mallie came rushing out of the farmhouse.

"I thought I knew that lovely laugh!" she said. "Oi, boys, don't be so rude to my guest!"

They went back to their invention, muttering about how girls knew nothing about vehicles.

"What do you want to do first?" asked Mallie.

I looked over to the stables.

"See how you get on with Mickey?" she asked.

"Yes please," I said.

"Well, bring your bag in and then we'll go over there."

Stepping inside the Lennox farmhouse was like being wrapped in a warm comfort blanket. It reminded me of what it used to be like in Holly Cottage, before we moved up to the big castle. It was a proper, jumbly, crazy family home, with random rollerblades here and there and tennis rackets and unopened mail and endless mismatching wellies. Bliss.

"Where are your mum and dad?" I asked.

"Oh, they're working with the sheep in the top field, so we can help ourselves to anything we like, Mum says. She's left us soup and bread for lunch, and she's making chicken fajitas for tea. And, wait for it, a giant pavlova!"

"Wow, delish!" I said.

I remembered Mrs Lennox's fabulous pavlovas well, and how she had to make double of everything because the boys ate so much.

There was a log-burning stove in Mallie's farmhouse kitchen, and it was a welcoming sight, with the farm dogs, Mr Punk (a spiky collie) and Thistle (a cute westie) snoozing contentedly in their baskets. It all looked so cosy and familiar. Mr and Mrs Lennox always cooked fresh food from scratch on their bright red Aga. As Mallie had said, there was a big pot of Scotch broth bubbling on the burner – and I knew they always made it just the way I like it, with lots of carrots, barley and peas.

"Mallie, it's lovely to be back!" I said.

"I know. It's been too long. There's so much to tell."

"Do you still do ballet, Mal?" I asked.

"Nah. There was this other young teacher who took weekly lessons for a while, and I tried it, but she wasn't the same," said Mallie. "And then she decided to move to Glasgow."

"Was she a bad teacher?" I asked.

She thought about this for a moment.

"Actually, no, she was fine. I think it just wasn't the same without you in the class," said Mallie.

"Aw, shucks, thanks," I said. "Do Mollie and Iona still dance?" I wondered, as I suddenly remembered two of the very talented dancers from Mrs Miller's group.

"No, most of the girls we danced with don't go to ballet lessons now. Remember Alice Marks, and Helen Hooper? They have both gone to boarding school at Glenalmond now. And Jane Bruce? She's really into acting these days. She's got an agent and everything. But I do know at least four girls who would still love to do ballet, like Isla, Mollie, Abi and Rachel. They would love to dance every week..."

I didn't say anything, but it got me thinking. When I originally wrote the plan for Cloudberry Castle School of Ballet, up in my teeny attic bedroom in Holly Cottage, I imagined that we *would* run weekly dance classes for local girls. In fact, Mum really wanted to open a ballet school because Mrs Miller was leaving. Maybe I should talk to Mum about the idea of having lessons for my old friends?

My head was buzzing with thoughts of the old days, but Mallie was keen for me to get out to the stables.

"Let's have a quick snack," she said, "And then we'll head out to see Mickey."

"Great."

There were two squishy armchairs at either side of the stove, and Mallie and I took one each. After a delicious glass of cold milk with a big slice of Mrs Mathers' oozy lemon drizzle cake, we headed out to the stables.

"Mickey will be hungry, so we'll get him to come over to the stable door by shaking his bucket of feed," said Mallie.

I nodded. For the first time, I felt a little apprehensive, and I recalled Mrs Mathers' warning about injuries.

14. Mickey's Great Escape

When we went out to the yard, Rory and Finn were still busily working on their flying machine.

"Hey, Katie, you're not going near that monster pony, are you?" asked Rory.

"Be quiet, Rory," said Mallie. "You're just a chicken."

"Yes, I admit I am, around that beast, anyway. There's no way you'll ever get that horse to calm down. There's too much damage been done to him already," said Rory.

"Well, I'm not giving up on him yet," said Mallie. "Come on, Katie. Just ignore him. You know what he's like."

Over at the stable, Mallie coaxed Mickey to the door as planned and he paced nervously, awaiting his food.

"Once his head is in the food bucket, I'm going to try putting the halter over his head, so we can attach the lunge rein for training. But he hates anything over his head, so don't panic if he goes crazy," said Mallie.

I stood back in the courtyard while Mallie performed this operation, which she had obviously perfected. When she put the halter over his head, he reared on his hind legs and neighed angrily. Peering into the stable, all I could see was his chestnut belly as he danced on his back legs, and poor Mallie's back as she struggled to bring all four legs back down to the ground.

"Don't worry," she called over her shoulder. "It's like this every time!"

"How long have you had him now?" I asked.

"For about four months," she said. "I know what you're thinking – that he should be better than this by now. Sometimes I wonder if I am ever going to settle him down. But I can't give up without a try."

"Yes, of course it's still worth trying," I said.

Finally, Mickey was calm enough to bring him into the yard, albeit on a very short rein.

I saw for the first time how gorgeous he was. He was just small enough still to be called a pony, not quite a little horse. He was very fine-boned and carried his thin legs beautifully, picking his feet up in dressage style. As well as the white blaze on his face, he had four white socks, which were, amazingly, exactly the same size on each leg. And I saw that he could have a beautiful coat, but it was very matted through lack of grooming.

"Oh, Mallie, he's so lovely!" I said, my heart melting.

"I know. But watch this. I'm going to try to get him to walk round in a circle at the end of the lunge rein soon..."

We went to the widest point of the yard, with Mickey pulling this way and that on the halter and short rein.

"Stand back," said Mallie. "I'm now going to let out the full length of the rein, and he might round about a bit."

Mallie let the lunge rein out bit by bit. At first, Mickey seemed not to realise that he had more freedom, and he stood still. Then it must have dawned on him that he could move naturally.

At first he just pulled a bit to the left and right. Then he bucked his back legs out in rodeo style.

Mallie tried her best to calm him.

"Whoa, Mickey. Good boy. No one is going to hurt you. There's a good boy..." she said.

But Mickey got more and more excited, and as

well as randomly bucking with his back legs, he began to rear up on his hind legs too. Even though he wasn't a huge animal, he looked very tall like that, and he seemed to tower over Mallie.

"Are you okay, Mal?" I asked.

"He's really bad today, Katie," she said. "This is my problem – I can't get past this stage."

I went towards Katie and Mickey. After all, I was there to lend a hand.

But I must have spooked him by approaching, because he started to paw the ground with his left hoof and his ears went back furiously. He suddenly stopped pawing the ground and his hindquarters were poised for action.

Just at that moment, Mallie lost concentration and dropped the lunge rein.

"Aaargh! I've lost hold of him. He's going to bolt!" screamed Mallie. "Look out!"

Before we could warn Finn and Rory, Mickey took off round the farmyard, cantering, then stopping to buck his back legs out.

"Oh no!" cried Mallie. "We'll never be able to catch him now!"

"Oh, I'm so sorry, Mal," I said, "I should never have approached like that. I don't know what I was thinking about."

"It's not your fault, Katie," said Mallie. "I dropped the rein and anyway, he's impossible."

"Why don't we get on our bikes and try to keep up with him?" I suggested.

"Okay, we can try," said Mallie.

Mickey broke out of the farmyard and headed for the paddock. He jumped the fence beautifully and landed in the paddock. We hoped he would graze at that point, but he kept running.

"He looks like he needs to run off all that tense energy," I said. "Why don't we just watch him for a while and see if we can read his behaviour. I heard about horses whisperers taming wild or difficult horses and you've got to spend ages observing them so that you know what has troubled them."

"Well, if you've got the patience, then that would be brilliant," said Mallie.

Over the next hour, we watched Mickey as he raced about that paddock, occasionally stopping to graze or drink water. He looked as though he thought someone was going to get him – as if he was being chased, but no one was chasing him.

"I think he needs to get rid of lots of energy

before we can start the proper training," I said.

"But what if he won't come back to us, even when he's tired out?" said Mallie.

"Don't think negatively. We're in charge of him, not the other way around," I said.

"Okay," said Mallie.

"Somehow, we have to let him know that he can trust us," I said. "Maybe we have to sit this out for as long as it takes, and wait until he comes to us for food. And even then, we shouldn't catch hold of him as soon as he has the food. We have to trust him in order for him to trust us back."

"Sounds good," said Mallie.

There was a horse shelter in the paddock, and Mallie and I sat in there, chatting about everything and anything, while we watched Mickey come to terms with the fact that he was safe in his new surroundings.

"Mallie, you go and get some food for him, and I'll wait here," I said after a while.

"Okay," said Mallie.

While she was back at the stable, I noticed that Mickey was coming closer and closer to the shelter.

"Hey Mickey, good boy," I said. "Come and see me, Mick. I won't hurt you, boy."

He walked right up to the shelter and looked in at me. I sat still. I wanted him to come to me, rather than me going to him, because being approached was obviously something he hated. We looked at each other. I wanted to throw my arms around his neck and tell him that he would be fine. But I just held his gaze and kept very, very still.

I was stunned when he took a pace towards me. Again, I sat still. Another step closer to me. Again, I sat still. I made soft reassuring noises, not even words, but sounds that he could tell were kind sounds.

Mickey came right up to me and nuzzled into me, with his vast inky eyes looking calm.

This time, I stroked his nose. He took a step backwards. "Katie, you idiot," I thought. "You've lost him again!" But he didn't go away completely. And we started the game again, of him coming towards me, little by little. I felt such a connection with Mickey, and I'm sure he could feel my love and patience for him.

This time, he came right up to me and pressed on my hands with his nose. I felt as though he was telling me that I could touch him now, so, without making any big hand gestures, I tickled his nose. He seemed to like it so I scratched the top of his head.

"Mickey, you and I are going to be best friends. And I will help you to have more fun. Because it's no fun being shut up in that little stable, is it?"

I knew from that moment that Mickey and I were going to have a special bond. Living and breathing ballet was all very well, but this was a magical moment.

Without me noticing her, Mallie had crept up to my side. She had tears streaming down her cheeks.

"Oh, Katie, thank you. You've done it! I've never seen him like this. Will you promise to keep helping me with him?" said Mallie.

"Of course," I said. "I've bonded with him now, and there's still a lot of work to do."

Mallie and I spent the rest of that Saturday, and the Sunday too, working on Mickey. We worked slowly, with a lot of watching and waiting. By Sunday afternoon, we had him walking beautifully in a circle on the lunge rein, and he could do this at a walk or a trot.

"Next step – a saddle!" I said.

"You really think so?" said Mallie. "I can't believe it. I didn't dare to dream that Mickey would act like a normal pony this soon. It looks like we'll be able to keep him after all. But only if you agree we share him?"

"Share him?" I said.

"Yeah. He belongs to both of us now," said Mallie. "And you can pop over here whenever you like to be with him, even if I'm not around."

I hugged her. "I've had the best time," I told her. "It's been totally magical."

I could not have been happier. How lovely to share a pony as beautiful and clever and adorable as Mickey. And to be friends with my Mallie again.

15. Velvet Crumples

I got back to the dorm, but then stopped outside the door of the room I share with Tilda and Catriona because I heard Velvet's voice inside. Velvet was in our room! I found that annoying for starters. But as I listened to what she was saying, I got even more upset.

"I think this suits me better than her," were the words I could hear. "What do you think, Tilda?"

"Yes, you look lovely in it," said Tilda. "Pink really works on you."

I couldn't quite figure out what they were talking about, but I was gradually getting the picture.

"These little ribbons and things are so cute," said Velvet.

"Yes, Katie did that herself," said Tilda.

"Well, anyone can do stuff like that," said Velvet.

"Yeah, I know, there's nothing to it," said Tilda.

At that point, I could stand it no longer and burst into the room, fizzing mad. My fury only grew when my suspicions were confirmed. Velvet was wearing my Sugar Plum tutu! The one I'd decorated myself! I could not believe the cheek of her.

"Anyone can do stuff like *what*?" I asked.

"Oh, erm. Ah!" she said. "I was just, erm, you know..."

"Please take it off," I said, in one of those controlled voices that would have been a big shout if I had lost it.

What made me even more angry was that Catriona, Eliza and Polly were in the room, entranced by what Velvet was saying. Not one of them had told her off for trying on my precious tutu. It was as if no one had the courage to stand up to her.

And Velvet did not take the tutu off. She carried on babbling to the others with tales of how many famous friends she had. She couldn't stop herself once she was on a roll. I felt like putting cotton wool in my ears.

"I've got so many celebrities on my mobile phone," she bragged. "But you know, they're just like you, except, obviously, way richer and they're famous..."

I could feel myself getting really fed up with her and just as fed up with my friends for hanging on her every silly word.

I cleared my throat. I was ready to sort Velvet Hughes out for once and for all – a job that, at the beginning, I had expected Tilda to do along with me.

"If you've really got all these contacts," I said, "then prove it."

"What do you mean?" she said.

"As I said, why don't you prove to us that you're telling the truth? Phone up some of these people who are so famous and who you apparently know so well, and let us hear their voices."

"Em, well, there's a time difference with L.A.," she said. "So that's a stupid idea. Anyway, I'm really insulted that you think I'm lying. Why would I need to lie? My father is a world-famous movie star."

"I'm sure we can work out the time difference and make some calls at the right moment," I said.

"I just don't want to call anyone, okay, Katie? Get it?" she yelled.

At this moment, Catriona grabbed her phone. "At least let us scroll down your contact list," she said.

Velvet pounced on her to get her phone back, but Catriona was determined to take a look.

"I'd love to hear the voice of a movie star or a movie star's kid," said Catriona. "Even if it's just voicemail."

"Look, give me the phone back," snapped Velvet. She sat down, and looked deflated. "Okay, so I don't *really* know as many famous people as I've said. The thing is, I feel under pressure to tell people what they want to hear about Hollywood. It's nothing like that when you live there." She burst into tears. "I hardly know anyone in Hollywood because my parents are really strict and don't want us to be spoiled and bratty. And here I am, acting all bratty, I'm sorry!"

I felt terrible. Why had I been so unkind? It was all because I had felt hurt about losing Tilda's friendship.

"Oh, Velvet, *I'm* so sorry," I said. "I didn't mean to hurt you. I was just annoyed at how everyone was listening to your stories, that's all."

"I'm glad you said what you did Katie, because maybe now we can all just be normal friends without me being special?"

"Of course we can!"

"Yeah, I don't mind a bit who you know or don't know," said Catriona. "I'm sorry you felt you had to be exciting all the time."

"Och, does this mean I can't come to a pool party in Beverley Hills?" said Tilda with a smile.

We all giggled.

"I'm sorry about all those silly things I've been saying," said Velvet.

"That's okay," said Tilda. "It's still awesome that you have a famous Dad and that you're going to be in a movie."

The girls in the room didn't say much but, one by one, they went off to do their own thing and from that moment we all accepted Velvet as one of us, and all the daft nonsense about Hollywood and celebrities passed over – thank goodness.

Velvet confessed to Tilda and I that she knew she wasn't picking up the ballet steps well enough.

"We could help you in the studio, without any teachers," I suggested.

"Would you do that?" she said. "That would be lovely."

"We'll go after tea every night," I said.

"Thanks girls," she said. "It really is much easier to learn from friends."

At bedtime that night, Tilda came over to apologise to me.

"I'm really sorry that I've been so in with Velvet, Katie," she said. "I've been an idiot."

"And I could have done more to understand how

Velvet was feeling. So, let's just forget it, shall we?"
I said.

"Okay!" agreed Tilda. "Oh, it's so nice to be back
to how we were!"

Tilda and I did feel almost as close as ever, except
that I held back a little bit of my heart this time, just
so that I would never get that hurt again.

16. Early Start

Tilda and I took Velvet down to the studio the next night as we had promised.

"Let's go back to basics," I said. "We'll start with the foot and arm positions and then try some pliés and port de bas. I'll just put some music on."

"Thanks!" said Velvet. "This is just what I need."

She listened carefully and did exactly what we said.

"Relax your arms, and tuck your thumbs in," I said. "That's good. Now Tilda will show you how to bend, while keeping your shoulders back and your bottom in..."

We carried on like this for ages, just doing simple routines. We had great fun, and at the end of the session, we all sat on the floor, chatting about ballet and tutus.

"I'm sorry I put your tutu on, Katie," said Velvet. "That was so rude of me. I was showing off."

"We all show off once in a while," I said. "Let's try out buns now!"

We sat in front of the huge mirrors and dipped into Mum's box of tricks. It was filled with clips, combs, clasps, grips, hairbands and nets. Velvet did a perfect high bun.

"Well done, Velvet," I said. "You look like the perfect ballerina with that bun!"

"Do I really?" she said proudly.

"What about mine?" asked Tilda.

"Erm, it's a tiny bit squint," said Velvet, as she adjusted it. "There that's better!"

Tilda smiled proudly.

I smiled too. I realised that Tilda really did like Velvet, whether she knew famous people or not.

The next morning, I set my alarm for 5.30 am, and jumped out of bed, washing and dressing as quickly as I could, especially as the heating wasn't quite on in the castle. As soon as I was ready, I ran down to the kitchens and made myself a big bowl of porridge with blossom honey. "I must be back by 7.00 am," I thought. "Otherwise, I'll get into huge trouble."

It was pitch dark when I sneaked out to find my bicycle and headed over to see how Mickey was doing. Since Saturday, I hadn't been able to think about anything else apart from Mickey. It had been the best feeling in the world when we made a breakthrough with him then, and I wanted to be sure that his confidence kept growing and he didn't just go back to his old ways. We still had to try a saddle on him, and then a rider, of course. It would be bliss when I could ride him round the paddock! My mind kept going back to how elegantly he had popped over the fence when he broke free. I think he's a showjumper.

When I got over to the farmyard, Mickey came to his stable door immediately. There were no wild eyes this time. He looked adoring, and those liquid chocolate pools of his made me melt. This time, I didn't restrain myself, I approached him softly, but placed my arms around his neck and he snuggled into me, making contented, whinnying noises.

"What shall we do today?" I asked him, as I undid the bolt on his door. "Shall we try that saddle on your back?"

I noticed that up close his coat was really filthy and full of dust and dander. So I looked around for grooming stuff. Out in the yard there was a tub filled with curry-combs, dandy brushes and hoof picks.

"Right, Mr Mickey," I said. "You're going to get a makeover!"

I lovingly brushed every corner of his coat and gradually a beautiful shine came over it, so that the chestnut gleamed like a newly fallen conker.

After that I began to tackle his matted mane and tail and that took ages because it hadn't been done in such a while, if ever at all.

Mickey seemed to love being pampered, and when I picked up his hooves to remove stones and other bits and pieces from his feet, I saw that they had outgrown his shoes. I decided to leave a note for Mallie. We had to get him re-shod as soon as possible.

The whole process of cleaning him up was such fun and I became completely engrossed in it. So it was a big surprise when I saw that Mallie, Finn and Rory were leaving for school! And I still hadn't got round to trying the saddle on him.

"Hi Katie!" called Mallie. "Why are you here at this time? It's quarter to nine."

"Oh no! Is it really?" I said. "Mum will be going crazy with worry! I'm in so much trouble!"

"Come round after school if you can?" suggested Mallie as she jumped into her Dad's filthy bashed-up old Land Rover.

"Yeah, okay, if I'm not grounded!" I said.

So much for my plans to be back before 7.00 am. I was dreading the reaction when I got home.

I kissed Mickey on the nose and jumped on my bike, cycling furiously back to Cloudberry. And I still had my lovely little Bella to check on too!

As soon as I got back, Mum and Dad came out to the courtyard to meet me.

"Where on earth have you been, Katie?" asked Mum. "We've been worried sick about you." Then she noticed that I had my jodhpurs and wellies on, and she sighed. "Oh Katie, you must be careful about doing too much with the pony over at Tullyacre. We have exams to prepare for here, as well as a possible opportunity to go to New York. And a pony that needs training is a lot of work for a girl who's already flat out busy."

I hung my head sadly. "Please don't make me give up Mickey," I thought. "I couldn't bear it."

Dad looked a bit more sympathetic.

"Leo is allowed to look after her pony," he said.

"Yes, but Katie has Bella to think of as well," said Mum. "She's going to get exhausted."

"Let her prove she can do it," said Dad.

"Well, I suppose so," said Mum. "But don't ever go away without telling us!"

"I won't! Thanks, Mum!" I said. "Now I just need to get changed and I'll be straight down to class. I promise I'll fit everything in!"

17. Good Fairy/Bad Fairy

Ballet class was lovely that morning. We covered the importance of mime.

"Ballet is an expressive art form," explained Willow. "And as such it is used to express emotions. Can anyone tell me what sorts of emotions we might convey in balletic form?"

A few of us put our hands up.

"Love."

"Forgiveness."

"Thankfulness."

"Hurt."

"Great," said Willow. "These are all super emotions. And they are things we feel. When we express them on stage, it makes the audience connect with us, and this is the true thrill of live performance.

I can assure you that when an audience get to their feet and applaud you and your fellow cast members for curtain call after curtain call, then there is no more rewarding sensation. Then you know that you have touched the feelings of a crowd."

We all faced into the mirror and practised making different expressive faces, especially using our eyes to get across particular emotions.

"This is fun!" said Catriona. "Look at my sad face... and now my happy face!"

"They're both the same!" I teased.

"Oh, that's so cheeky!" she said. "That was my best acting!"

"You're doing really well, girls," said Willow. "But I have one idea that will help us to be even more expressive!"

We were intrigued, and watched as she went to fetch a huge box with a handle, a bit like workman's toolbox.

"Now, what do you suppose I have in here?" she asked.

"Tools?" suggested Polly.

"In a way you're right, Polly," said Willow. "Tools of a ballerina's trade... But can anyone be a bit more specific?"

"Is it props, like you have in a play?" suggested Leo.

"Also an interesting answer, but just not quite right," said Willow.

I put up my hand. "Is it make-up?"

"Yes, it is!" said Willow.

"That huge box is full of make-up?" said Tilda.

"Yes, it is!" said Willow.

"Crikey. That must be a lot of make-up! Can we look in there?" asked Tilda.

"You can do better than that," said Willow. "We are all going to try expressive make-up looks!"

"Yahoo!" said Tilda. "I love make-up!"

Willow began by demonstrating two looks. A good fairy, which was Eliza, and a bad fairy, which Willow did on herself – perhaps thinking it would be a bit rude to single any of us out as a bad fairy!

We all watched with wonder, admiring the pinks and gold applied to the good fairy, and the blacks and dark greens and purples for the bad one.

"Maybe we should try out make-up techniques in case we get to audition in New York," I said to Polly.

"Yes, *Nutcracker* make-up would look just like that good fairy!" she said.

"Well, I've got lots of make-up in the flat, so we can try that later, okay?" I said. "I've even got glittery stuff!"

"Cool!" said Polly. "We can all try it."

"Yes, that will be fun!" I agreed.

I spent the whole day thinking about how amazing it would be if I got the chance to travel to New York, and see the exact place where Mum had trained, before I was even born.

By teatime that night, I was shattered. Thank goodness for Mrs Mather's scrumptious meals. We had fish and chips with lots of peas and ketchup, served with freshly baked bread and butter, plus sticky toffee pudding with the smoothest pale yellow custard that was ever made!

I went to see Mrs Mathers afterwards.

"Tea was delicious, thank you so much," I said.

"Oh, Katie, just doing my job," she said with her lovely warm smile.

If fairy godmothers do exist, then Mrs Mathers certainly is one.

18. News from New York

At lunchtime the next day, Mum asked for Leo and I to visit her office.

"Do you know what this is about?" asked Leo, as we tapped on the door.

"No, I have no idea," I admitted. "But I don't think we're in trouble, are we?"

"No, not that I know of," said Leo.

"Come in," called Mum.

When we went inside, Mum was grinning from ear to ear, so we knew it wasn't anything terrible.

"Take a seat, girls," she said.

"What is it?" I asked.

"I have some lovely news for you two. The New York City Ballet would like both of you to travel to New York and audition for the part of Clara!" said Mum.

"Wow!" said Leo and I in unison, and we hugged each other.

"That's awesome. I can't believe we're going to New York!" I said. "Will you take us?"

"Yes, of course I will," she said. "And Sorcha will come with us too."

"So when do we go, Mrs Mackenzie?" asked Leo.

"Right, I have the email in front of me here," said Mum. "You are to go there on June 6, along with another six girls from the UK. The successful girl will go to London for two weeks before Christmas for rehearsals and three nights of performances, before the ballet company continues on to Paris where a French girl will dance the part of Clara."

"Wouldn't it be amazing to dance on the stage in a real ballet?" I said. "That really is my ballerina dream!"

"Well, I will be thrilled if either of you get the part," said Mum. "And I know it will be disappointing for the other girl if one of you is lucky, but I have already decided that I will take all our girls to see the ballet in London, no matter what happens. I'm sure your mother will be thrilled, Leo."

"Yes, I know she will be delighted about this," said Leo. "What do we have to do to prepare?"

"I have a note of the dance they want to see. A simple sequence depicting the spirit of Clara, that's all they're asking for," said Mum. "We will make sure that we display a good range of technical features, but the role will not require pointes. Do you have any questions, Katie?"

"Yes. I wonder if Mallie will cope with Mickey while I'm in New York?" I asked.

"Katie, it will be a great opportunity for Mallie to do some more work with her horse. I was rather hoping for a more ballet-inspired question," said Mum. "This is such a thrilling opportunity for you."

"Sorry, Mum," I said, with a laugh. "It's great news – really it is. I could not be any more thrilled. You're right, thank you. I can't wait!"

I cycled over to see Mallie after school, to tell her about the New York trip.

"Oh, that's great news, Katie," she said. "Well done!"

"It's not for too long, but obviously I won't be able to help with Mickey while I'm away. But you are getting much better with him now," I said.

"Not exactly," she said anxiously. "I find it much easier when you're around."

"Let's see how you get on with him just now. I'll stand back this time."

"Oh, that's a good idea, Katie," she said. "I need to bond with him a bit more. And with you going away, I really must get down to it."

"Well, let's get this boy out and see what mood he's in," I said.

"Okay." She stood back to let me go in for him.

"No, you lead him out today," I said gently. Maybe I had been doing too much and had been a bit possessive with Mickey.

Mallie looked nervous about this idea, but she walked slowly toward the stable.

Mickey looked at her suspiciously and then he looked across to me, as if to say; "What's going on today?"

"Act a bit more confident, Mallie."

She charged into the stable.

"Not *that* confident!" I called.

"Make your mind up!" she said.

"Let's stay calm, or he will never settle," I said.

When he came out of the stable, Mickey looked really agitated.

"You take him, Katie!" she said.

"No, he's fine. Hold him and soothe him. Tell him he's wonderful. He likes that."

She took a deep breath.

"Good boy, Mickey," she said. "I love you, you are so clever..."

"That's good! Now, get him to stop, and tie his halter rope to the hoop while you get the tack."

"Whoa, boy," she said. "Good boy, wait here, that's a good horse. Lovely boy. You're doing well!"

She went off to get the tack and Mickey stood nicely awaiting her return.

Maybe I was a tiny bit sad that Mickey was being just as good for Mallie as he was for me. But that was a selfish feeling. She was doing a brilliant job and I realised that I had not given her enough time with him. Now that I was going to be away for a while, it was great that she and Mickey were working well together.

"It's okay, Mickey," she said. "I'm just going to put your saddle on. You'll be fine..."

And he was fine.

After watching Mallie and Mickey getting on famously round the yard, I cycled home with a tear in my eye. Maybe I had wanted Mickey to rely on me. The time had come to let go a little. After all, he wasn't my horse. However, I would not give up seeing him. I loved my times over at Tullyacre Farm.

When I got back to Cloudberry, I went straight to see little Bella, the pony who had been with us on the estate since I was little. I threw my arms around her neck. "I'm sorry I've been neglecting you, lovely Bella," I said. "You are my very own pony, and I will always love you!"

19. Hard Work

I carried on spending time with both Mickey and Bella, when I could get away from ballet lessons, and I found that I didn't have much free time. Life at ballet school is never boring but it can be really tough. It was all exam timetables, hard work on technical steps and ballet history. We all knew that we had to work hard if we wanted to succeed.

"Girls," said Willow. "You can only have the easy times if you put in the hard work as well. I promise you this phase will pass and there will be lots of fun to come."

Much as I loved Willow, I was starting to find her classes a bit less enjoyable. It was all about accuracy rather than interpretation now.

One morning after an early start with Mallie

and Mickey over at Tullyacre, I trudged into ballet class in the studio with heavy feet.

"Katie Mackenzie!" said Willow. "Let me see you walk like a ballerina! We do not drag our heels along the ground. We glide with elegance, or bounce with excitement."

"Sorry, Willow," I said. "I'm just so tired."

"We all get tired, Katie," said Willow, just a little more sharply than usual. "But where ballet is concerned, we have to simply put it first."

I took that to be a reference to the fact that I had been spending lots of time with the horses lately. There was a cheeky little voice in my head, saying: "There's more to life than ballet, you know!" But I respected Willow so much that I took her comment seriously and began to think about it.

When it was my turn to try a battement frappé, my coordination seemed to disappear. There I was, with all eyes focussed on me and I could not remember how to do such a move. My right leg, instead of doing controlled leg movements, seemed to tremble and wobble about aimlessly.

"I've forgotten how to do a battement frappé," I wailed, dissolving into tears of exhaustion, sitting down on the floor with my head in my hands.

"Katie, relax," said Willow softly. "You're just panicking because you're tired."

"Please may I sit this out, Willow?" I asked.

"No, Katie. You may not. We have to get this exactly right!"

I dried my eyes and stood up, partly angry, partly determined.

"Good, Katie!" said Willow. "Let me see your fighting spirit. Ballet is about perfection and perseverance. I need to see that in you!"

I stood by the barre and tried the frappé again. This time I got it precisely right, then when it was over I fell down again with exhaustion. But again, Willow was not having it.

"Get up Katie!" she said. "Sauté please!"

My fifteenth attempt at a sauté was the one that finally satisfied Willow and after that she left me alone. We had never seen Willow quite so steely before and, much as I found her rather scary in this mood, I had to admit that once I had done everything perfectly, I would never forget how to do it.

Ballet was relentless and there wasn't as much praise going around. At least the ponies didn't blow hot and cold with me – they were sweet and steady the whole time.

20. The Ballet Exam

When spring came to Cloudberry, a carpet of green was polka-dotted with tiny white snowdrops. The trees began to come to life and the sun tried its best to warm the old castle, trickling in through the windows. Velvet had settled into life at school, and it was decided that she'd stay right up until summer, as her dancing was finally coming on well, helped by Tilda and I practising with her most evenings.

It was really tense at Cloudberry as exam time approached.

Madame Jennifer Capers, the examiner, seemed a bit of a dragon at first. She arrived in a taxi from the station and we all went to the window to look at her. She wore a heather-coloured tweed suit and sensible black patent-leather shoes. Her hair was set in a grey cloud, in a style which was so old-fashioned it made the Queen's hair look stylish. She wore pearls and pale chalky face powder.

"Oh, hello, Madame Capers," gushed Mum.

"Hello," said Madame Capers.

"How was your journey?" asked Mum.

"It was acceptable," said Madame Capers.

"Can I offer you any refreshments?" said Mum.

"Some Darjeeling loose-leaf tea with lemon would be very palatable, thank you," she said.

I've decided that people who use big words where little ones would do are just pathetic, so I was put off Madame Capers from that moment.

When I was called into the studio for my exam, I didn't know what to feel. I was nervous of course. But I told myself that if I flunked it, I could always become a full-time groom at a stable and eventually open my own riding school. However, as I danced through all the technical steps, Willow's brilliant training kicked in, and I found myself dancing my socks off and getting every step just right.

"Very nice," I heard Madame Capers mumble. "Lovely footwork..." She jotted notes down on her sheets of paper.

With those words of encouragement, I put even more effort into every step, and I felt as though I was dancing on my own at Cloudberry Castle before we converted it into the dance school, when this studio was a dusty old ballroom and there was just an old-fashioned record player and huge black disc records for music.

"Good work, Katie!" said Madame Capers at the end of the exam.

Mum stood proudly in the corner, beaming a "well done!" smile.

After the exam I was enjoying ballet again and I still loved all the pony jobs, but I was getting worn out with the work I was doing round the clock. When the alarm went off at 5.00 am each day, I felt as if I'd only just got to bed. One day when Mum was giving us instruction on the role of French concert culture in the development of modern ballet, I am ashamed to say that I fell asleep in class. She let it go, but I knew I couldn't continue like this much longer without a big ticking off from her and Dad.

One Saturday in May, I arranged to bring Mickey over from Tullyacre and go out for a hack with Leo and the Duke. We saw some members of the local riding school out as well. As we cantered along, Mickey got it into his head to jump a gate up ahead. I held onto him as tightly as I could and went with him. He cleared the gate with no problem. It was a great feeling, to be in the air on your pony, soaring over a tall gate and landing safely on the other side. It was magical, like flying. As we turned round to try it again, one of the riders from the riding school group approached me on her bay mare.

"Have you ever thought of entering the local showjumping contest on that pony?" she asked. "He's got a great jump and you've clearly got a lovely bond with him."

"Oh, that would be fun," I said. "But I don't have time. Maybe the owner of the horse would like to though."

"If she comes by the riding stables on the Perth road, I'll give her an application form if she likes," she said.

"Great, thanks, I'll tell her," I said.

The lady went off to rejoin her group.

"Don't tell me you'll want to start a riding school next?" said Leo with a giggle.

I bit my lip. I had even had that thought myself.

She had a good point. It was as if I was getting as much into ponies as I had once been into ballet. I still enjoyed ballet, but what if the ballet school had just been a childish craze, and now I had landed everyone in the family with the idea?

21. New York City

I was rehearsing the Clara dance every day for our audition trip to New York. Of course I was thrilled that I was invited to audition for *The Nutcracker* and that I was going to travel to America, but I was going to miss Tullyacre, Mallie and Mickey.

As spring at Cloudberry changed into early summer, the date was fast approaching for Leo and I to head off on a flight from Edinburgh airport to JFK in New York. It would be lovely to have some time with Mum, even if Leo was coming along too. And, of course, Sorcha was part of the group. There's no way we could go to auditions for Sorcha's favourite ballet without the little snowflake herself.

Leo and I practised our dance routine for two hours every evening in an extra class with Mum.

This meant that I had to stop doing extra work with Velvet, but Tilda and she carried on dancing, and sometimes we all met in the studios.

"You doing battement tendus and pirouettes again?" Tilda would say.

"Yep, and are you doing ronde de jambe and port de bras again?" I would say.

Leo and I were getting on really well, and even though she was very competitive about getting the part of Clara, I tried not to think about how I'd feel if I lost out to her. There was no denying that dancing in *The Nutcracker* was my ultimate dream come true and I could feel some of my old ballet ambitions come back again from time to time.

It was curious that, even though both Leo and I were learning the same dance for the Clara part, it looked completely different when she did it, due to our different expressive styles. Leo was technically very brilliant, whereas I was more free and easy. As Mum said, it would just depend whether either approach was what the Director of Ballet in New York had in mind for the role of Clara in their particular interpretation.

I spent ages deciding what I should take to wear for the audition and for going around New York as well. Mum said it would be warm and maybe a little humid. I was excited about seeing the Statue of Liberty and Central Park, but I knew that we had a tight schedule.

Mum had a lot to arrange so that the school would run smoothly while she was away with us. For the few days we were away, she had increased the academic lessons and decreased the amount of ballet, which meant that Leo and I were unpopular, as we were causing extra maths and geography classes.

Sorcha helped me to decide on what I should take, as ever. We got together in my room a few days before the trip.

"What should I wear for the actual audition?" I asked.

"I think you should wear something a bit like what Clara would wear," suggested my little sister.

"That's a good idea. What do you have in mind?"

"Well," she said. "I have printed off a picture that I think might give us the right look."

"Let me see," I said.

She presented me with a gorgeous image of a girl in a pretty Victorian-style party frock, just like the one that Marianna Cappaldi wore as Clara in the Scottish Ballet production. It had cream frills and a longish full skirt.

"Oh, Sorcha, you're so right!" I said. "That *would*

be lovely! But how am I going to get that in time for our trip?"

"Well, I hope you don't mind," said Sorcha, "but I mentioned it to Mrs Renton when she was babysitting for Hamish and me the other night, and she's already made it for you!"

I couldn't believe it. She ran off to her room and came back with a beautiful creation on a coat hanger.

"I just want it to go really well for you, Katie," she said. "And I know you've been a bit more interested in Mickey than in ballet recently, but I think ballet is still your best thing!"

I ran to hug her, then I tried on the dress and danced around the room like Clara, trying out the steps I'd been rehearsing.

The last thing I did before heading to the airport was rush over to Tullyacre. I kissed Mickey on the nose and hugged Mallie for ages.

"I'm going to miss you, Katie," said Mallie. "And so is Mickey."

"But you and Mickey are a team now. Did you pick up an application form for the local showjumping competition?" I asked.

"Yes, I did actually," she said. "I'm a bit nervous about entering though."

"Oh, but you must," I said. "He's a natural over fences and it will really help you two work as a unit. Promise me you'll do it."

"Okay, Katie. Just for you."

The final goodbye at Tullyacre was a bit sad, even though I knew I'd be back soon.

Eventually, it was time for Dad to drive us to the airport to catch our flight to New York. It was a much bigger plane than the one we flew to London in, but Mum said it was not the biggest there was, because Edinburgh airport couldn't fit the hugest ones on its runways.

Leo and I did puzzles and watched films all the way across the Atlantic, and Sorcha watched too and did some colouring in, while Mum flicked through her magazines. It was much faster than I thought it would be, and before we could blink, we were peering out of the windows at the Hudson River and the Statue of Liberty.

We landed at JFK International Airport. We were really in New York!

22. The Audition

We took a yellow cab to our hotel, which was amazing. It was called The Grand, and Mum told us we were very lucky to be put up there as guests of the New York City Ballet, because it was an expensive hotel, and it certainly did look it. Mum had organised for our room to overlook Central Park, as I had been going on and on about wanting to see it. When we arrived it was almost bedtime, and Mum said we'd have jet lag and should get a really good sleep for the next day – which was AUDITION DAY.

As I lay in bed, trying to get to sleep, I whispered to Mum, "I think I've forgotten the whole Clara dance!"

"You'll be fine, Katie," she said. "Your brain will remember it no problem at all, I promise you. Just relax, get some good sleep and your ballet instincts will take over."

"Yeah, I'm sure you're right," I said.

Next day, after a scrumptious breakfast of pancakes with syrup, we set off for the auditions. Mum knew her way around the area well from the days when she had danced with this ballet company. She first met Dad when he came over here to test out New York delis and write an article about them. So this was a very much-loved city for her. I could see her get in her stride as we negotiated the few streets that led us to the huge building where the ballet was housed.

We were met at reception by a young dancer who was very friendly. She introduced herself as Norah.

"I can't believe I'm actually meeting *the* Beth Berry," she said, looking at Mum. "I saw you dance when I was five, and it's because of you that I am here today. You inspired me so much. You were the most graceful dancer I have ever seen. It was magical to watch you."

Mum blushed from the neck up. "Oh, how sweet of you!" she said. "That's the loveliest thing anyone has ever said to me!"

"Well, it's all true," said Norah. "Anyway, this is all about these two lovely little dancers now. Let's go and see where you will dance, and you can get changed and warm up. How does that sound?"

"Great, thanks," I said, and Leo agreed.

She took us through a maze of doors until we came to a huge dance studio. It was lined with mirrors and barres all the way round the edges and the floor was made from light wood. The coolest thing was that the whole roof was glass, so there was masses of natural daylight flooding into the room.

"This is where you'll dance," said Norah. "We'll run through the music with you as many times as you like. You will be filmed, so that we can watch you over and over again. Part of what we want to get a feel for today is how you will respond to other dancers on the stage, so we will bring in our principal ballerina, who will dance the Sugar Plum Fairy in the production. You'll love her – she's called Alicia Primrose."

"Wow, that sounds great!" I said.

"Can't wait to meet her," said Leo.

We got changed into our dresses. Leo's was lovely too – her mum had sent it up from England and it was pale china-blue, with frills and a dark-blue velvet ribbon round the middle.

We listened to the music through once, and then began to warm up at the barre for our solo performances.

Just as we were stretching our legs and arms, a vision fluttered into the studio.

It was Alicia Primrose, dressed as the Sugar Plum Fairy! She travelled in on pointes and made her way over to us. She was so pretty! She had peachy skin, and her fair hair was piled in a high bun. Her tutu was made from sparkling pink tulle – there were tiny diamonds stitched all over it. She carried a silver wand with her and she waved it above Leo and I. "Hello, girls," she said. "Thank you for coming all the way from Scotland for this audition. We only chose those girls who we could really imagine coping on a great big stage. So have confidence: try not to worry about your dance. Just dance for pleasure."

Leo went first, and Mum and Sorcha and I watched in wonder as she gave a faultless performance.

"How do I follow that?" I mumbled, as I began to stretch and warm up for my turn.

My mouth went dry when the music began for my audition piece. The musical introduction played and I tried to relax. I thought very hard about the spirit of Clara and how she would feel if she were at the centre of this adventure.

The dance came back to me automatically, and I did my best to think of Decembers in Holly Cottage, and the excitement of present giving and the spark of wonder in the air that Christmas always brings.

All my steps came easily; the pliés weren't wobbly and the pirouettes were faultless. My body took over from my brain and I was immersed in the act of dancing; nothing else in the world mattered. I felt like my body knew exactly what to do and had limitless energy inside. I felt excited and elated as all my hours of hard work were combined in this perfect moment. At last the music stopped and I curtseyed. Whatever happened after that, I knew that I had never danced so beautifully.

Mum could not say much in front of Leo, but I could tell by her smile that she thought I'd done well.

Now it was time to explore the life of a famous ballet company!

We were taken to the costume department.

"Look, Katie!" said Sorcha. "There are at least ten Sugar Plum outfits! And some of them are tiny!"

Norah overheard her.

"Hey girls, if you want to do some dress-up, then that's fine by us," she said.

"You mean we can try on the actual tutus and everything?" I asked, incredulous.

"Yeah, sure," said Norah.

I chose a very sparkly pink one, a bit like Alicia's, except even more glittery. We then picked out tiaras and wands. Once I was all dressed, I couldn't resist dancing around the dressing room in the role of the Sugar Plum Fairy. I knew every step from the performance we'd seen back in the New Year at the Festival Theatre in Edinburgh.

Then the Director of Ballet came to see us. She looked very elegant and although her face was stern she had gentle eyes. She wore a pale grey dress that hung from an empire-line waist.

"How do you do?" she said, looking at both me and Leo. "I am Calista Du Bois, Director of Ballet here, and I have so enjoyed watching your performances just now. There is something very special about each of you and I can imagine that a glittering career lies ahead for you both.

"Thank you!" we chimed.

While Mum caught up on news with Calista, the dressing-up continued. We had a ball in that dressing room, and my delight in ballet came flooding back.

Ballet is my *first* love, I decided.

23. A letter

When we got back to Cloudberry, I knew I had to make a decision about the amount of time I was spending on Mickey. I went to check on Bella, who looked like she was in good form; her coat shone and her eyes sparkled with excitement at seeing me. Then I headed over to Tullyacre, wondering if Mallie would be a nervous wreck. I shouldn't have worried. She had set up a jump course in a paddock, and she and Mickey were cantering through it like experts.

"Hi Katie!" called Mallie. "Look at us! We're in the horse show on Sunday too!"

"Wow! That's brilliant," I said.

I was proud of the two of them. It looked like they had bonded even more since I'd been away and, although there was tug at my heart because I felt so close to Mickey, I knew it was right for him to be settled with Mallie now and that I was free to focus on my ballet.

When Mallie brought him over to see me, he nuzzled into me and I threw my arms around him.

A wave of relief came over me. Mickey was going to be just fine, even if I could only work with him once a week. I hugged him. He would always be special to me, but my ballet had to come first.

When the summer holidays came around, we had to say goodbye to Velvet. We threw a garden party for her, and Mallie and some of the girls from Mrs Miller's old ballet class came, as well as some mums from the village and all the students and staff from the ballet school.

Mallie and Tilda did cartwheels together in the sunshine and Mum organised a huge game of the Grand Old Duke of York. We all fell about laughing, just as Mrs Mathers arrived with some of the other staff, carrying big picnic baskets. While she spread out the picnic rugs, we grew impatient to see what goodies she had made. There were all kinds of sandwiches, and golden pies, as well as fruit salad, nachos with dips and as for the cakes! There were iced fairy cakes, strawberry tarts and chocolate brownies – and everything washed down with Mrs Mathers' home-made lemonade.

It was so nice to have all my friends, old and new, getting along together.

After the picnic, Mum tapped her glass with a spoon to get everyone to quieten down.

"Can I have your attention girls, please," she said. "I want to announce that, as from August, I will be running weekly ballet classes here at Cloudberry for non-boarders!"

"Hooray!" everyone cheered. At last my local friends and my new ballet school friends would be together. It was such a nice feeling to have them all united.

During the summer holidays, I heard that I'd passed my ballet exam with distinction, just as I'd hoped. And then a letter came. I read it once. And then again:

NEW YORK CITY BALLET
THE LINCOLN CENTRE NEW YORK NY 10023

August 6

Dear Katie,

Thank you so much for attending the audition here in New York for the youth outreach part of Clara in our travelling production of *The Nutcracker Suite*. It was a pleasure to meet you. We enjoyed your dance greatly and would be delighted to have you take the role of Clara for us in London and contribute to our international development programme for young dancers. You will be required for three of our matinée performances.

Given our longstanding connection with Beth Berry, and our interest in Cloudberry Castle School of Ballet, an accompanying letter asks your mother whether she would allow us to base ourselves at the castle from November, so that you can rehearse in your familiar surroundings, and we can contribute to the work at Cloudberry for the mutual benefit of all. We hope you are as excited by this proposal as we are.

A contract, schedules and other administrative details accompany this letter, and please do not hesitate to call with any queries.

Yours sincerely,

Jane Howe

Senior Administrator
NEW YORK CITY BALLET

And the lovely thing was that Leo had got a role too, as an angel, which was a beautiful dance, and she was completely thrilled as well. After all the painful hard work, and the times in term when I had felt so frustrated with ballet, this was a lovely turnaround. It made me feel as though creating the Cloudberry Castle School of Ballet had been a success after all.

24. The Performance

At the end of the summer, we heard that Velvet's *Sugar Plum* movie was going ahead and that the director was really happy with her ballet work. That was a lovely feeling after we had all put so much effort into helping her. She sent emails to us all the time telling us about the filming.

With the new term, Mum's weekly lessons for non-boarders started. It was such fun when my old village friends came to Cloudberry, especially Mallie, who rediscovered her love of ballet. But even though she started to dance again, she still found time to win rosettes with Mickey on showjumping courses all over Perthshire! I was so proud of them.

In the autumn we prepared for the New York City Ballet arriving for their rehearsal time at Cloudberry.

Dad got lots of extra rooms painted and carpeted and when they finally arrived, we were caught up in a whirl of rehearsals and mealtime chatter. Everyone loved having the guests at the castle, because it meant that we had no routine, and every day was exciting. They taught us dances and we were allowed to watch rehearsal time for the corps de ballet and even the prima ballerinas. Alicia Primrose was a lovely dancer and she was also kind and approachable and did not show off at all. She was simply a dedicated dancer who wanted to be the best she could be. Tilda, Catriona, Polly and I sat with her at dinner one night, and got chatting to her.

"I almost gave up on ballet when I was your age," she said.

"You're kidding?" said Polly.

I was all ears.

"Yes, it's true. I couldn't decide between ballet and swimming, but swimming was making me too exhausted for ballet, so I had to let go of one of them. I spent a whole summer thinking about it, and I nearly went with swimming..." Alicia told us.

"And what made you decide on ballet?" I asked.

"Well, I was swimming that summer and I thought to myself, I can always swim no matter what, but if I pull out of ballet school, I'm unlikely to dance ever again," she explained. "And I still do love to have a swim, but I just fit one in from time to time."

"I see what you mean," I said. And it was the same with horses. I could always potter around stables, but if I lost the ballet habit, I would never get it back. There was no doubt that I was a ballerina through and through and that all my ballerina dreams were coming true. I danced and danced and danced until I perfected the role of Clara. I was going to perform on the stage like a true professional – just like my Sugar Plum Fairy inspiration from the New Year, Marianna Cappaldi.

Mum and Dad took everyone from Cloudberry to London to see Leo and I perform, including some of the local girls who came for weekly classes. We had such fun on the flight from Edinburgh. In fact, we almost took over the entire plane. Then we all got the express train into the city and arrived at our hotel: Edwards – the same one mum had taken Sorcha and I to when my ballerina dreams properly began, the time we went to see *Swan Lake* at Covent Garden.

It was our final performance when the girls from Cloudberry and Lochvale were in the audience. I was determined to make them proud of me, as was Leo. I was very tense backstage.

"Are you okay, Katie?" asked Leo.

"Not really. I'm so worried that I might mess up tonight," I said.

"You won't!" said a voice. But it wasn't Leo's voice. It was a man's voice – a familiar old man's voice. It was Dr Campbell!

"Dr Campbell?" I whispered. "Are you still looking after us?"

"Yes, I am, because you have looked after my castle. Keep dancing, Katie," said the voice.

"Katie? Katie? Are you imagining things?" said Leo.

"No, not at all," I said.

I jumped up. "I'm ready for this now."

"Let's get into the wings, then," said Leo.

When I was called forward, I held my head high and became Clara. As I danced over the huge stage, I had no sense of being Katie Mackenzie from Perthshire. I really was Clara. And when the audience broke into applause, I knew that I was living out my ballerina dreams. And as I looked out to the audience, I saw Mum, Dad and Sorcha. And Mallie, Catriona and Tilda. All my special people.

After the performance, there was a knock at the dressing-room door.

"Come in!" I called.

The door opened.

It was Velvet!

"Katie, I just had to see you!" she said. "You helped me dance beautifully for the film. But you are the real ballerina. You will be the best of your generation!"

"Oh, Velvet, that's a lovely thing to say," I replied. "That has always been my dream."

Read more of Katie's ballet adventures in two other books!

Katie Mackenzie loves ballet, and longs to be a ballerina like her mum. When her family inherits an old castle, Katie dreams of turning it into the most wonderful ballet school in Scotland. That's if she can stop her parents from selling it. With a little mischief and some help from her friends, Katie sets out to save Cloudberry. But the castle has its own secrets, if only Katie can unlock them before it's too late.

e Also available as an eBook

Cloudberry Castle

Ballet School Secrets

Cloudberry Castle School of Ballet is finally open, and Katie's dreams are about to come true. She can dance all day, make lots of new friends, and be taught by a real ballerina from the Scottish Ballet. Then spoiled brat Leo arrives, with her pony and private chauffeur, and Katie's dreams turn sour. Will Leo out-dance Katie to play the principal role in the Christmas show? And will a ghostly presence lead the girls to uncover more of the castle's hidden secrets?